The Dawn
An Alaskan PAW Novel
Book 3

Copyright 2012
Publisher: R. E. Stowell
Fairbanks, Alaska

Aspire to lead a quiet life, to mind your own business, and to work with your own hands, as we commanded you, that you may walk properly toward those who are outside, and that you may lack nothing. 1 Thessalonians 4:11-12

A prudent man keeps his knowledge to himself, but the heart of fools blurts out folly. Proverbs 12:23

Cover photo by Rosalyn Stowell
Photo of the author by Samantha Stowell
Technical Advisor - Mark Massingill
Researcher - Kara Stowell

This is a work of fiction. Names, characters, places and incidents are either the product of the author's imagination or are used fictitiously and any resemblance to any actual person, living or dead, business establishments, events or locales is entirely as a part of the fictional story. If you recognize yourself in these pages, you have a vivid imagination and should be writing novels, yourself.

For thus says the Lord:
"The whole land shall be
Desolate;
Yet I will not make a full end.
For this "shall the earth mourn,
And the heavens above be
Black,
Because I have spoken.
I have purposed and will not
Relent,
Nor will I turn back from it.
The whole city shall flee from
The noise of the horsemen
And bowmen.
They shall go into thickets and
Climb up on the rocks.
Every city shall be forsaken,
And not a man shall dwell in
it."
Jeremiah 4:27-29

Prologue

Just after I cross the last large bridge, my pickup has some steering problems and I almost go off the road. I slow way down and proceed with extreme caution. As I proceed, I see that several trees are down along the road that I didn't noticed before. These are close enough to come get for firewood. I turn my radio on, just to see if maybe that was another earthquake. All I find is static and dead air. That is not unusual with my radio and I think nothing of it until I get closer to home and as I start past Will and Shari's, I see them outside, sitting on the ground, holding each other. Something is wrong so I pull in.

Shari is crying and Will is upset. This does not look good. "Is it the baby?" I ask as I stop.

"No, Bubble Bump is fine. But I think the rest of the world is in trouble." she replies.

"The early reports are of massive damage and loss of life all over the world," Will says.

They have been using a broadband radio he bought a while back and are monitoring the short wave stations. None of the usual stations are on the air. He says the reports out of the Anchorage bowl area say there is no more Anchorage, no more Seattle, no more cities left standing around the world. Major fires from ruptured pipelines. The underground facilities everyone thought were foolproof and completely safe have either collapsed or flooded out. Whole countries are no more. Islands have disappeared and a few new ones have emerged only they used to be inland mountains. There is speculation that possibly 2 or more of the countries developing nuclear weapons may have detonated at various places at about the same time and set off worldwide earthquakes of a magnitude beyond the Richter Scale.

I want to stop and check on Kara and Rose before going on home to see what damage my place may have sustained.

I pull into their driveway and see that Roman's cabin and buildings seem to be okay. I go on down the hill and the guest cabins seem to all still be standing. Kara's house looks okay from outside. I stop and go to the door. No one answers so I go on down to her Mom's. Kara is there and we go inside. Rose is fine and picking up a few items that had fell. Nothing major seems to have happened and the house looks okay. Kara says her place is fine, also. I tell them about thinking my pickup is breaking down. We laugh but it is not much of a laugh.

If Fairbanks didn't get hit very hard, soon there are going to be thousands of hungry people looking for food wherever and however they can find it. I tell them what I heard at Will and Shari's. There was no mention of damage to the Interior city or towns. We are far out of town, but not that far if they still have fuel to drive. All the military bases are a worry, also. That is a lot of people needing food in the immediate area.

Since it is late August, the nights are starting to get fairly dark again for a few hours. None of this is good news I have to get home and see what damage I have and how my animals are doing. As I pull into my yard, I see a stranger sitting on my steps waiting for me. When he sees me, he places his hands on top his head in a classic prisoner pose. He holds this as I walk toward him with my handgun in my hand. "Who are you and why are you here?" I ask.

"My name is Jeremy Rhodes and I killed Rod and Rob before they could hurt Shari. I caught your goats after the quake and put them back in the pens. I've been keeping an eye on Will and Shari's place since Royal and his buddies showed up. I don't want to hurt any of you but I really, really need a meal and someplace to stay, if possible. I know you should just turn me in, but honestly, I won't hurt anyone here."

Strangely enough, I believed him. It had to be someone they knew, to get close enough to each guy and knife them while they waited in ambush for Will and Shari. I asked him exactly what happened that day, then said "Wait, why don't we go over and let you tell it to everyone here and we will decide what to do. After I check in the house first to see if everything is okay.?

He said he checked under the house and it looked solid and okay. So I unlocked the door and he went in ahead of me. There were some pictures off the walls and a few items fell from shelves in the living room, but overall, it looked pretty good.

We stopped at Rose's and she and the guys and Kara followed us over to Will and Shari's. Shari was shaken to see Jeremy but hugged him saying she knew he wouldn't hurt her. Seems he is her cousin.

Once we were all introduced, we waited for the story.
Jeremy started right from when they left the airport. He only came along to be the calm voice of reason, he thought, so the couple could talk over some legal matters needing cleared up by the death of Shari's folks. They did not think Rod was all that bad, and left him some property jointly with Shari, in their Wills with Rights of Survivorship. Rod

decided he wanted it all. But Jeremy didn't know that until he was tied in the back of the SUV and heard what they were planning. He was to take the blame and they were going to use her own rifle to shoot her and if they had a chance, Will, also. Rob was only backup and to make sure Will didn't show up too soon after Rod had his little talk with Shari. Jeremy finally managed to work loose from his bonds while they trashed the house. He went in as they were going out the back and they did not see him. He found the large sharp knife where they stuck it into a sofa back. He followed Rob first and came in behind him as he hid behind the old outhouse. He was making too much noise to hear Jeremy, who had been in Special Forces in the military, slip up behind him and slit his throat without a sound. He quickly stuffed him into the outhouse and then stalked Rod. He found Rod just as he was taking aim at Will. He wanted to taunt and punish Shari, so he was going to shoot Will right in front of her. The other woman (me) being there didn't even slow down his plans. He figured he would get to punish 2 women instead of just one. Jeremy slid silently up behind him and stuck the knife up under his ribs just as he started to squeeze the trigger and the rifle went off. There wasn't time to hide him or the rifle as we started directly for the sound of the shot. Jeremy just had time to get himself hidden before we got to the body. Then the Trooper showing up really made it impossible to do anything and Jeremy was afraid they would haul him in and he would never see the light of day again.

Well, since the earthquake, we had no idea whether or not there were any Troopers left to come out or if there were any type of Court system left in the State. We talked it over while Jeremy sat in the other room, and decided he probably had saved several lives by the 2 he had taken. If Will and Shari were willing to have him stay here, the rest of us had no problem with that. They were willing. He was very surprised when we told him the decision.

Then talk turned to the earthquakes and Will turned the shortwave radio back on for us to hear the updates. There were still a few HAM operators on the air and trying to let everyone know the extent of the damages. It sounded like the earth as we knew it was totally gone. There may still be a few small towns and villages here and there, but the roads, trains and shipping was gone. All the major cities? Also gone. It was hard to think that Fairbanks may be the largest city left on earth. It had no means of supporting itself, so it soon would cease to exist as a city, also.

I finally got home and unloaded my pickup.

It would probably be the last load of anything I would ever be able to buy in town, ever. This was it, there won't be any more. Noah helped me put the feed away and unloaded the building supplies and rugs into the barn.

We are both silent as we part and he goes back to his camper which weathered the quake fairly well.

The next morning, we awaken to a freak snowstorm. There is about a foot of heavy wet snow on everything and more coming down. Oh, this isn't good for the survivors in town. If they have no electricity most won't have heat. As deep and heavy as the snow is, no one will be driving out this way, anyway, so maybe it is good news for us.

The snow continues all day and there is the crashing of tree limbs breaking from the load on limbs still covered in green and gold leaves. Trees are bending and the brush is almost flat on the snow banks. The wind has come up, so it is blowing drifts across the roadway, also.

I ask Noah if he wants to try making it over to be with his Dad and brother. He says no, he is comfortable where he is, but if it gets much colder, could he move into the little cabin out back? It does have a small wood stove in it. Well, yes, it would be nice to have him here.

The snow keeps falling and during the

night, the temperature starts dropping. I feel sorry for anyone out in this weather and the poor folks without homes now are to be prayed for.

Early the next morning, I hear the sound of a snow machine coming in my driveway. It is the fellow we delivered firewood to, this summer. He comes to the door and says he is just checking to see if I am okay and is going over to check on Rose, Kara and the new folks. He asks about the earthquake so we tell him what we have heard on the radio at Will and Shari's. He is dumbfounded and just shakes his head. I ask him if he will be okay and he says yeah, he has over a years supply of gas for his snow machine and chainsaw and seldom ever went to town, anyway. I send him on his way with a bag of cinnamon rolls to either keep or share at each stop he is making this morning and invite him back for a meal on his way home. He accepts after thinking it over a second or two.

After he leaves, Noah comes to the door and I let him in. He has shoveled a path from the house to the barn and to the woodshed. I fix breakfast and he is very happy to come in and get warmed up and a hot meal. After breakfast, I start bread dough and a large pot of stew from the remnants of the garden.

I gear up and go out to care for the goats. They are enjoying the snow. I think after a while they may get tired of it just like most humans do. At present, I am thinking it may be saving us from some unpleasant encounters with town folks. Maybe by the time they decide to head this way, they won't have fuel for the trip. Right now, the only way they could reach us is by snow machine and they would have to be hauling extra gas for the trip.

Late afternoon, the guy on the snow machine stops back by to let us know the latest news from the other direction. He found everyone warm and cozy and at Kara and Rose's they were even happier. Their kids and "adopted" in town had rounded up some motorcycles and trailers right after the earthquake, loaded up all they could find and came home. They got to the place just before the snow hit too hard. They said the bridge was out just north of town and they came through the river. The next bridge was cracked and they went over it one at a time, being very careful, the lightest loads first. Then at the last large bridge, they again crossed in the river as the bridge looked like it was not safe, to them. Town had been hit harder than the reports stated. The underground utilidors under the Bases and under downtown Fairbanks had all collapsed and no utilities were working. The runways were all buckled and broken. No flights could enter or leave, except helicopters and only if they had enough fuel in the tanks as the tank farm was on fire. The roads going south from Fairbanks were clogged with traffic thinking they could drive somewhere and get away from the disaster. No one was headed north but them.

Both of Rose's great grandchildren made it out with their parent. Their community had increased, but Rose and Kara both planned on them being there in emergencies, anyway. Some of the little extra cabins were just for each adult to have their own place. The "adopted" ones were also welcome and also had been planned for.

We shared our meal with the man and he accepted another bag of rolls and some bread to take on his ride home. He left soon after and we were glad he had stopped by. That was the best load of firewood we ever delivered.

Noah and I sat and tried to figure out exactly what was going to happen next and how to deal with it. We know we could survive out here, if we are left alone. It sounds like Wasilla may now be ocean front property. So the coastline has changed drastically. I am wondering how Interior is going to change if the ocean levels are rising or have risen. Most of the Yukon and Tanana valleys are not very much above sea level. What if we now could catch ocean fish just down in our valley? We will probably have to wait until the coming summer to find out about that.

4 months later:
Well, it is the end of the old year and what a year it has been. The world has come to an end, as we knew it. As far as I can tell, there will be no commerce or government as such, any time in the foreseeable future. Whatever supplies we have on hand in anything, is going to have to last, and last, and last. There will be no running to the store if something runs out. We are going to have to find alternatives for just about everything. If not for ourselves, then for our children and grandchildren.

In some ways, the future looks grim, in others, maybe the best that could have happened to us.

There have been murders, there have been new lives enter our sphere. There will be more in the future. It is human nature.

I am going to get married sometime in the spring. That is if we can wait until spring.

Almost 2 years have passed;
We have survived a couple of attacks, found fuel supplies at the Yukon River

Bridge, Noah and I got married and I have a baby girl.

We are not aware of it until later, but Rose's sister and family and friends from Oregon are currently wintering at Delta 100 miles south of Fairbanks, with a herd of cattle, horses, some chickens and turkeys they have traveled almost 3000 miles and spent 3 winters camped, with. They have shared cattle and knowledge as they traveled and during the winters, helped establish a couple of communities.

Thad and Kara seem to have an understanding of some sort and get along very well indeed.
Roman and Rose may or may not have. They enjoy working together and spend a lot of time together, but both also enjoy their own company.
Kara's adult children each have someone in their lives, but have not totally decided on what they want in the future. Her grandchildren are a joy to everyone there.
Jeremy and Ashley are doing well in their marriage. They would like to have children, but so far are not putting that as a priority.
Will and Shari are enjoying their twins so much and doing very well in their marriage.

He is everything her first husband was not. A truly loving husband and partner.

Dan, a trapper on the Porcupine River flew in with his plane and we now have another member in our community. He married Melanie, a friend of Sam's that came out with her.

Dan and Melanie will soon have their child. They have some problems, each is so used to being on their own, they don't think about the other person first. They are both trying to do better and now are focusing on the child soon to arrive and trying to put it's welfare ahead of what they want to do. Their marriage is indeed a work in progress.

Al and Natalie now have a fine little boy. He was born a couple of days ago. Farren is becoming a happy young man and adores Natalie and the baby and thinks Al knows everything worth knowing. He is learning how to be a good hunter and trapper while not over harvesting the area he uses.

We are all doing pretty good and are looking forward to summer.

Chapter 1

I open my eyes to my favorite view, the lovely melted dark chocolate eyes of my husband, holding our incredibly adorable daughter. Okay, that sounds pretty sappy even to me and I love them both. Yes, he is holding her, yes, she is adorable, but she just pulled over the pan of water and has saturated the floor and the hides we were working on last night. She is cooing her cutest smile up at him as though she is very proud of her accomplishment and he is about to let her get away with it. I softly mention, "If it would still be cute when she is 16, then let her get away with it now."

He looks a little guilty, then sternly tells her "No" and starts cleaning it all up after putting her into her little pen.

She looks surprised then sits down and starts playing with her rag puppy toy I made for her. It used to look sort of like a sock monkey, now it is mostly a dingy rag toy.

With all the spring chores starting, we are having a time keeping her in sight and out of danger. So we take turns cutting trees and working on the firewood.

Now that we have more gasoline since finding the tanker, we can use the chainsaws and the pickup and are making the most out of it. I think everyone is. The sound of spring out here is the sound of chainsaws out in the woods.

When the boat was brought out from town and the guys picked up supplies at the boat shop, they brought all the stabilizers and oils so we had lots to mix in and keep the fuel better longer. Then the extra supplies we loaded up, from the old shop at the Yukon Bridge helped out a lot.

Yes, we are feeling positively wealthy with all we still have. It is going to take a lot of work on everyone's part, but with care, we can survive and thrive out here. The greenhouses are all ready to plant, the gardens will be, as soon as the snow is all gone. The goats and chickens are increasing, especially the chickens. The caribou are doing well, even. They don't respond to voice commands but are okay if someone leads them, and they will pull a sled with a fair load on it. The dogs are learning to pull their sled very well. They love to run and pull so we use them as much as possible.

Our little trees that Dan flew in from the nursery in Fairbanks have mostly survived. I have the different mints planted in beds around the yard to keep them separate. They make such wonderful tea and flavoring in syrups and jelly. The apple trees, we espaliered against the barn and woodshed walls to give them protection and a bit of warmth and just maybe keep the moose from eating them too much. I put the 2 plum trees against our house and the 2 cherry trees, also. I planted some of the berry bushes between the trees, hoping the reflected warmth from the house would help them, also and not sure whether moose would eat them or not.

Al was first to plant his trees that way and it sounded like a good idea. His were thriving, also. Maybe in a few more years we could be picking fruit. Even my seedlings are growing well but who knows just what type of fruit we may get from them? Any is better than none.

While I am daydreaming about fruit, Noah has the mess pretty well cleaned up, just one more reason to love him. When I finally surface, Elaine has her arms up, wanting out of the pen. Okay, straight from the pen to the high chair. Breakfast time and it isn't going to be a chase the baby around the house to stuff a bite in now and then breakfast. She looks disgruntled, but oh well.

Once breakfast is over, we bundle up and head over to see Kara and Rose. This may be one of the last runs with the dogs and sled this season as the snow is getting spotty and we are on the roadbed almost as much as we are on snow. The dogs enjoy it anyway since they aren't hauling a heavy load. The team is growing as we add puppies from last season's litters. Some show promise of being good work dogs and a couple may work out as leaders in the future.

When we turn in at Rose's driveway, the dogs recognize where they are going and pick up speed. We enter Kara's yard at top speed and do a loop around her circular driveway. What a bunch of show-off pups.

One of the young men that came out with Kara's son has managed to hurt himself and is getting repaired down at Rose's place. She isn't actually trained in any of this, but she has some common sense. She cleans out the cut on his arm and then super glues it together. A bit of bag balm over it and a bandage to keep it clean and sends him back up.

He is feeling a little ill to his stomach as he had to assist in his own repairs. He will probably be a lot more careful in the future. Injuries can be bad at any time, but now, the chances of infection are always present and it can be a life threatening occurrence. No one here has any type of antibiotic. Everyone out here is relying on natural herbs and oils. Some are very effective, and usually no side affects, but not something anyone wants to check out. He said he did cough a little to see if she would give him some of her homemade cough syrup. She didn't buy it.

We visit for a while, then go on down and see Rose. She laughs about the fake cough. She gets a lot of that.

Then we go see Roman and Thad, Noah's Dad and brother. They have spent an interesting winter. Roman is working on a generator system using a wood gasifier he put together from assorted parts. He also did some wood working over the winter in his shop trailer. He made some cribs for all the new arrivals showing up in the community.

As we head for home, the dogs try to veer off the trail after who knows what. Noah manages to get them back on track and we stop to investigate. There are tracks in the snow that look like someone on snowshoes. But why would they be off in the woods breaking trail when the roadbed has a well used trail on it? We would not have noticed it, if the dogs hadn't. The tracks are headed toward Rose's place.

We turn the team and go back to let Roman know and he can tell everyone else. He is surprised to see us back so soon. We tell him about the tracks and he sends Thad to Kara's and he heads down to let Rose know. They both are armed. He worries about her, she worries about him, but they are both too stubborn to get any closer to each other.

Once again, we start for home. When we turn in our drive, we notice a small piece of cloth fluttering in the breeze in the brush by the main road. It looks like some type of signal and we remove it. When we get to our yard, it is obvious someone has looked the place all over.

Somehow, this does not feel like a friendly little look see. We check out the goats and chickens. They seem to all be accounted for. The caribou are out in their large pen and seem nervous, but they always seem nervous, so it is hard to tell. Nothing is out of place around the outbuildings and yard. But there are snowshoe tracks everywhere.

Noah wants to backtrack the person and see where he came from. We don't know if male or female but the tracks look fairly deep so probably a large man. I want Noah to go get Jeremy. He used to be in Special Forces and is excellent at what he did. Finally Noah agrees and I take Elaine in the house and lock the doors as Noah leaves.

After Noah has left, I am a nervous wreck. When it was just me out here, not too much bothered me, but having a child and a man I love now involved, it really gets to me. All of the what if's. I keep a gun handy and one in the back of my waistband. I have another stashed in the back of the couch where Elaine can't reach it. I have my razor knife in the top of my boot. Another in the diaper bag.

So when I hear a knock on the door, I am ready. When I open the door and see a sweet looking little old lady standing there, I invite her in. As soon as we are in the house, she pulls a nasty looking gun out of her coat and holds it on me as she starts toward the door to unlock it for her partner. I can not let that happen. When her eyes leave me to undo the complicated locks we have, I ease my own gun out and pulling it into position as she turns to check on me. I shoot her.

There is a loud pounding on the outer door as I yank the gun from her hand. I check the window and do not recognize the person pounding on it. So I exchange my handgun for a 12 gauge shotgun and open the window a crack.

"What do you want?" I yell out the window and the man whirls and is drawing a weapon as he turns, so I shoot him, also. The woman seems to be coming around a little bit, although I think she won't last very long. She tries to talk and is saying "Frank, Frank" as she breathes her last.

Elaine is screaming from the earache the guns in the house have caused, some woman that looks like Mrs. Santa is dead and bleeding all over my floor and some guy named Frank is dead or close to it on my steps. So I take care of my daughter.

After she is calms down, I put her in her pen and drag Mrs. Santa out the door. Frank has breathed his last and made a mess of my steps while doing it. For a day that started out so fine, it has not gone all that well.

I clean up the mess indoors as well as possible. I am scrubbing the floor for about the 4th time on my hands and knees when I hear someone outside. Not again.

This time I check out the window and have a gun in my hand as I check, just in case. Then, even though I can see Noah, I still have the gun in my hand as I unlock the doors and let him in.

He grabs me in a hug and is looking me all over to make sure I am okay, then he looks at Elaine, watching us with her big eyes rounded. "I can't leave you alone for an hour without you getting into some kind of trouble, can I?"

"Well, she started it." Is all I can think of to answer back.

He goes back out and loads them on the sled and the dogs are set for another run. He is going to take them around and see if anyone recognizes them. He returns in a couple of hours with an empty sled and no one has a clue who they were. Frank was wearing a large pair of snowshoes that matched the prints all over the place and Mrs. Santa had stashed a smaller pair beside my door. I couldn't ask them if they had tied the cloth on the bushes at our drive to signal others or if it was just for themselves. Another worry, just what I needed.

Chapter 2

Down in Delta Junction, Liz and her family
and friends are getting ready to start the move
north. They knew no one was expecting
them and there would not be room for all the
animals they managed to make it this far with,
so they were very generous with the amount
traded out to the folks around Delta.

They hoped to find more survivors along
the way, but couldn't count on it.

They could be proud of all they
accomplished in one winter at Delta. From 2
factions fighting with each other, they now
had a nice little community, working pretty
well together. It was decided the large barn
used for the winter programs would continue
to be a community center and school.

There was plenty of grain left to plant
enough fields to supply all their needs and
have some left to trade. With the wood
gasifiers built over the winter, they would
have tractors to do most of the planting and
harvesting.

Chickens and turkeys now were part of
every farm. If they were taken care of and

properly handled, there should be enough next year to have a few meals from them besides the eggs.

Loading the wagons required a lot of planning and deciding what had to be taken, then what was just wanted to be taken and if any room left, the things it would be nice to take. Another wagon was added to make sure most could be taken with them.

They planted a garden for the other folks to use, before leaving. It was up enough to supply fresh salads before they left.

Finally the grass was growing well enough to supply the feed needed for travel. The remaining cattle and horses were herded together and started north. The worst obstacle north was the river crossing of the Tanana where the pipeline used to cross. The ice looked stable and they crossed the wagons one at a time across. As the last wagon pulled up on the far shore, the ice started cracking. Now the herd was on the south side of the river and the wagons all on the north side.

The bridge looked okay, but no one was willing to trust that it was. Finally, one old cow decided to check it for them and trotted across. It held, so they let a few cross at a time, until all the animals were across, also. Then the riders crossed, one at a time. There were cracks across the road surface and as they crossed, the cracks widened. No one wanted to go back and check.

A lot of the cows were calving as they progressed, so they took it slow and easy for the new calves. Some days not even 10 miles were made. Two weeks into the trip, they were nearing Fairbanks. As they neared the old Air Force Base, they saw signs of people, but no one came out to investigate what they were doing. They posted guards for night watch and as it didn't get dark, it was easy to see if anyone tried to sneak up on them.

They are willing to share, but giving or trading is one thing, thieves are another. During the night, they caught two thieves and tied them to a tree by camp.

The following morning, a group of people approached the camp, calling as they came in. Richard and Mike met them at the edge of camp.

"Uh, we seem to be missing a couple of our young men." One finally says. Another is tugging on his coat and pointing to the two being chewed by mosquitoes, tied to the tree. The leader reaches for his weapon but Liz suggests they not do that as she and the rest have them covered very well.

"Now we can sit down and talk and see why you thought you needed to steal from us."

The whole group sat down and looked sullenly around. While they sat there, a young woman came walking in from out in the trees.

She came over to Liz with her hands held out at her sides to show she wasn't going to do anything stupid. "I told these idiots to just come in and ask if we could trade for some cattle, but no, they had to go all macho and just try to take what they wanted. We have some items to trade, if you will trade."

The men looked on, some sullenly and some brightened up a lot at the sight of some food being brought over for them. It was simple fare but good and filling.

After eating, they got down to trading. They had a lot of military gear from the Base and wanted to get some cattle and if possible a couple of horses to raise on the farmland cleared across the river near here. They were amazed at the tractors running on wood gasifiers so were shown how to build their own. Some bags of seed grain were included in the trade and they soon left as happy new farmers. The two thieves would be reprimanded when they got back home. Liz thought the night sitting in the mosquitoes was probably quite a punishment.

Now they were all outfitted in nice military clothing and had plenty in the wagons to last them quite a while. The best part was all the winter gear and socks. Socks and underwear were priority items.

They were very close to the former little town of North Pole and wanted to check and see if the Church they had attended over the years was still standing and if anyone was around there. They were very happy to find a few friends still there and the Church in use as a center to distribute help and excess supplies. The folks at the Church were thrilled to see what Liz and Richard had to share with them. The next day being Sabbath, they stayed and held services in the Church and a nice potluck after that raised everyone's spirits.

There were several families in the area trying to farm, so they stayed a week, helping set up a wood gasifier from materials found in the area and an old tractor one of the families had. They left a couple more bags of seed grain to be planted for crops. They told them about the group out near the Air Force Base. In future, they could trade back and forth.

They wanted to get entirely through the town area of Fairbanks in one day, so started out from North Pole and camped only 10 miles farther. The reports were that the Wendell Street bridge was standing in good shape, so they planned on herding right on through on the east side of town and crossing there.

They made it through town in good shape and stopped near the building supply stores to check and see if there was anything they could salvage. There were a couple of people there, so they offered to trade some cows for some building supplies. They were able to get some boxes of nails, some spikes, and some concrete pier blocks. The metal roofing and roofing screws cost them a horse. But when the woman came around the corner and discovered they had chickens, she made them include several rolls of house wrap and more roofing in exchange for a few hens, a rooster and 2 turkeys. She wanted eggs. Liz included some fertile turkey eggs for the hens to brood that were broody. They didn't care what type of egg they were on, just so they had eggs.

By the time they reached the far side of town and found an area they could spend the night, a few more folks were coming around to see what they could trade. One couple came by and told them it used to be dangerous to be out in the open here, but last winter, the rough group that considered themselves above the bounds of decency disappeared and no one is missing them.

Now everyone is trying to work together and make a community again. They are rebuilding their greenhouses and would have produce to trade later in the summer.

When they started out the next morning, they didn't have so many cattle or horses to worry about feeding for the coming winter. They did have a lot of building materials, and grain from Delta. There were still a lot of chickens and turkeys in their cages on the trailers.

The grass was growing well along the road right of ways, so the cattle and horses were content to graze their way north. Finding areas to bed them down for the night was more difficult up in the hills past town.

As Liz and Richard used to visit ever couple of years, they were familiar with the terrain and distance yet to travel.

Chapter 3

Back out here, we are doing some checking on where these people came from and if they were just a couple, or if there were more of them around.

There were more of them.

Guess they thought Rose was the weak link over at her place. She was cooking dinner when they broke in through her front door. She calmly invited them to eat, then seasoned the stew from one of her herb bottles in her pantry. In case that didn't do it, she acted like she was putting a certain bottle out of sight, like it was something special, which it was. The men grabbed it, held it up and looked at it and sniffed it. It smelled like sweet berries and alcohol. They started passing it around as they ate. Rose quietly backed out of the room as she didn't know how fast the stuff worked or if they would have time to hurt her when they realized what was happening to them.

Some got outdoors before keeling over, the cramps wracking them as they lay on the ground, a fine froth forming at their mouths.

The largest man was the last one down and he did realize what was happening. He tried to get his gun out and his eyes to focus on his intended target. Rose wasn't holding still for that and managed to get his gun away from him. She kept prodding him to make him crawl outside. Finally she got in front of him and taunted him enough he kept lunging forward until he was out the door and in her yard with his men. Later, she said she didn't want to have to clean up after them all in her house. It was bad enough to have to dump all the food where no animals or birds could get it and wash up the dishes and pots. The food was dumped in the outhouse.

Rose locked up her house as best she could and walked up to see if Roman and Thad could give her a hand. She had a bunch of trash needing hauled away. They looked perplexed but willing to lend a hand. She suggested the pickup or to borrow Noah's front end loader we brought down from the Yukon River area.

She stopped and told Kara on her way back down the hill. Kara walked on down with her. They searched and stripped some of the clothes from the bodies.

They found a hand drawn map with each of the places along the roadway marked on it and notes beside them on the map. Someone had scoped us all out pretty well.

I hated to think someone watched us that closely and no one noticed. It is really hard being alert to danger all the time and still get anything done. There aren't enough of us close enough together to really manage to keep a guard out all the time. Now I know how the early settlers must have felt when they had to carve out homes in wilderness and watch for someone sneaking through the brush to stop them.

I really hated the idea that someone watching our place decided I would be a sucker for a sweet little old lady and let her in. Which I did. Even though she looked like Mrs. Santa, she resembled Ma Barker even more. I feel like a sucker, so they must have pegged me right.

This group appears to have come down the road from the north. We are not sure if they are from Manley, farther out the road, or just assorted people that banded together from along the haul road. We don't even know if there are still more of them.

When we go check on Al, he says he has been doing some target practicing the last few day and teaching Natalie and Farren how to shoot better. Maybe they decided to leave him until later. He saw no one.

Chapter 4

We did very well on the birch syrup making this year. Lots of sap before the nights got too warm. I even made quite a bit of candy from it to save for the winter holidays. If I want to try making sugar of a sort from it, we can always pound it to a powder and use it.

When I mention that to Roman, he makes me a nice deep birch mortar and pestle to pound it in without scattering it around so much. This is great, I can use it to make seasonings from dried herbs. Not the ones Rose used in her special stew the other day.

We get on with the gardens and greenhouse planting, and sowing the grains we have. We shovel out the barn as it thaws and clean out the chicken coop. The dog yard cleanings are kept separately. We are composting it and hoping to use it scattered and raked in on the grain plots. We will only do a small area in case it doesn't turn out so well. Everyone always says not to use dog or cat poo, but we get so much a year, it should be good to use on something. I wouldn't want to use it in the greenhouse or the garden, but will try it out on other things.

We have managed to clear enough area for planting grain, that we try tilling some of it to till in the dog fertilizer. It is rough going and we managed to find a lot of rocks and break a shear pin. Since we don't have replacements, we use a large nail and bend it over. If we do that again, we will probably break an axle.

For the other plots, we make a drag with spikes sticking out on the bottom and hook up all the dogs to pull it around, breaking up the surface of the soil. It is like a miniature chariot race, with the dogs running full out and one of us trying to stay on the drag to give it weight and control the dogs.

Thad shows up just as I take a good tumble off the back of the drag and stands there clapping. I sit up and call Pal and he comes back all happy. At least I won't have to chase the drag all the way down the hill to catch them. Then I throw a rock at Thad.

Kara is standing behind him and she is snickering, so I throw another rock, which also hits Thad as she ducks and pulls him around in front of her. Oops.

The dogs happily follow us over to the barn to be unhitched. They have earned some treats so I give them each one as I unhook and snap their leads on. Pal is the only one allowed loose and in the house. They all gobble up the salmon snacks I bake for them.

It has a little bit of everything we have on hand in it, and they love them.

The grass is growing fairly well now and so are the weeds in the garden. We spend most of our time on the garden and greenhouse since we already have the woodshed full for next winter. We are considering building another woodshed farther from the house, and filling it also. We worry in case of a fire, would we lose all our firewood also? We have other buildings including the ice house that we could live in, but only one large building full of firewood. I would really hate to have to start cutting and hauling firewood in the winter to use as we cut it.

Noah and I start building another woodshed. It won't be any farther from the house, just on a different side. We have so much practice building these from helping on everyone else's, that we have the walls all up before anyone stops by. Then Thad and Roman come over and help Noah roof it. We use old salvage stuff I have on hand until it runs out and Roman brings over some he salvaged on one of his stops at the Transfer Stations when he was bringing out supplies before the quake.

Of course an empty woodshed must be filled, so we start in on that. With the sap up in the trees, the wood is far heavier than it is in early spring. We leave enough space between rows for air circulation to allow the wood to dry and not start rotting on us.

Roman's next trip over, he has news, very big news.

Rose's sister, Liz and her family and some friends and neighbors have arrived from Oregon. They have trail drove a herd of cattle and horses up and brought chickens and turkeys, also. We are going to find places they would like and start building again. They have seed grain and we will need to clear a lot of area to grow enough hay for all the animals. They want everyone interested to come get some.

We fuel up my old pickup since everyone north of us pretty much knows who it belongs to. We are to go see if anyone within 20 miles or so north would like some animals to raise.

We are in luck. The first people we find are Steve and Dani and Boy 1. He is a sturdy looking little guy and it looks like Boy 2 or Girl 1 is about to join him soon, when we see Dani. She just giggles and says she decided to quit waiting for Steve to have the next one. They never did agree on a name for Boy 1, so would let him pick one out when he gets older. They are excited to find they could get a couple of cows and some chickens. The goats I gave them are doing very well. They will let everyone else in their area know and be over in a couple of days after they build a corral and start clearing ground for hay.

We head home and stop and see Al. He would like some more chickens and a couple of turkeys, he isn't sure about cows.

So far, the brush and downed tree fence around Rose's place is keeping the cows and horses fairly well in place. They had to quickly build fence around gardens and the spring head.

A couple of days after arriving, they took most of the herd back down to where the barriers had been placed across the valley to keep marauders from town away from us or at least impede their progress. With a few additions and replacing what was taken down to get the herd through coming this way, it makes a nice fenced area of a few hundred acres.

There was a shallow valley just the other side of Dan's place, that faced south, but no one had ever lived up on it. A road of sorts was quickly cut between Dan's place and Will and Shari's place to access near the middle of the valley. Then Rose used her dozer that Roman had repaired to clear the valley of most of it's trees, making large berms to act as fences around the outer perimeter. Near the head of the valley, quite a ways up the hill, she leveled off a nice large area that looked out over the whole valley. She left a fringe of trees to act as windbreak and give shade in the summer. Even before building, it looked good. Seed grain was scattered as soon as the ground was cleared and a drag used to smooth it out as well as possible. We just hoped it had time to grow before freeze up. Since it was early June, it should.

Next came building a house. They had brought a lot of building supplies from town and we had a lot. Roman had enough to build several homes but had bought it to build for he and his sons. He said he was enjoying his little cabin too much to build another as long as Rose didn't mind him staying where he was. She didn't mind. Noah and I certainly had what we needed as a home. Thad said he was happy to continue as he was. The way he and Kara smirked at each other, I think they like things the way they are, also.

So, Roman brought over the backhoe and dug down to rock to backfill with more rock for their foundation to set on. They took the loader down and brought back buckets of gravel to put all around the yard and driveway. Then more buckets of rock to backfill with.

While the backhoe was over here, they dug out a small trench from the little creek and put it right along the edge of the yard, then let it find its way back down the hill. More gravel was hauled to line the trench with, along with larger rocks. An area is prepared to build a large barn and closer to the house, a nice woodshed. They liked the way Roman had his outhouse and indoor plumbing arranged, so planned on that, also. It would save steps in winter. With the outhouse near the back wall of the house and indoor plumbing emptying directly into it and a vent pipe from the outhouse up to the roof of the house to keep odors out makes it very handy. I wish mine was that way.

Everyone starts hauling over building supplies while Liz and Richard decide just what they want to build as their home. For the time being, all their family will be living with them until places can be set up for each family. They are considering making some smaller cabins and everyone coming to the main house to eat for now. That would give privacy and everyone their own space. It is working well at Rose's. Rose shows the extra folk picked up in Canada how they build the Trapper cabins and says if they want, they can just pick a spot and build, anywhere along the road. They are welcome to come for meals.

Mike and his family want to settle beside Liz and Richard and they go a bit farther down the valley. Rose fixes an area with her dozer just like the one she did for Liz. She places the building site up on the side of the creek above the area so they can see out over their large field, also.

While Rose has the dozer working in the area, she clears a field for Dan, then one for Will and Shari and another for Jeremy and Ashley. There will be a lot of feed needed for cows and horses this winter.

Roman digs out new outhouse holes in the area for the ones that want one ready. We have no idea how long the fuel is going to stay good and the dozer and backhoe are both running good right now. The front end loader is used hauling gravel and rocks until everyone has a nice stockpile on hand.

A few of the cows seem gentle enough to try milking. None are actual dairy cattle, although some may have a bit in them. We need to build stanchions to hold their heads in place before any serious milking will get done.

They had picked up several Scottish Highlander cattle in Canada and kept them all to bring out here. These are some furry cattle and should winter very well here. We need to build shelters of some sort for all the animals. At least 3 walls and a good roof over it for rain and windbreak. Since hay will be limited, we probably should build in feeding troughs also to prevent waste.

After the people up the road come down to see about getting some cattle, there are still over fifty head to try wintering over. Plus the horses. The 2 teams are definitely needed to stay. Several of the riding horses would be very nice to keep. So we will try to make sure there is enough grain and hay to see them through the winter. Next winter, we should be old pros at this.

I think I can keep some of the turkeys over the winter in my barn. We keep a fire going for the goats most of the winter in it, anyway. Liz had let one of her broody hens set on some of the fertile turkey eggs as they were traveling up from Delta and they are about to hatch. We put them in our little mobile chicken coop and start building another one.

The hen is a large very hefty hen, but when her "chicks" hatch out, she looks at them a bit oddly, but they are her dear babies and she shelters and mothers them. Those are going to be some mixed up turkeys.

This summer is more hectic than usual. We are trying to make sure everyone will be settled and have food and wood for the coming winter. Jeff and Lela are settling into a small Trapper Cabin between Rose and Jeremy, so is Leif. Sara and Tina want to stay near Liz and her family for now. So a small cabin is built for her. The young man that joined the group at Haines Junction wants to build a nicer place between Rose and Jeremy's places. He wants to convince Sara that she and Tina would have a good life with him.

Rose fixes a nice area for him as she is taking her dozer home. After she leaves his new place, she makes a few more building areas with nice sized yards, along the road, just in case. Some on each side of the old road bed. They may grow back up before anyone needs or wants them, but in the meantime, they will grow more grass to be cut as hay. Hay is going to be a priority for quite a while.

By the end of June, the grain is coming up very well in all the fields. The foundations are built for the main big houses and several of the little cabins have sprung up around each place. Later, they can be used for storage, if no one wants to live in them.

Chapter 5

Everyone still has gardens needing weeded and kept watered and greenhouses. By the time we get some sleep at night, we are all bushed. No one is going to be fat by the end of this summer. Not that anyone is, now, anyway. Nothing like limited rations and hard work to keep a person in shape.

The quinoa is doing great with the added animal fertilizer being used on it. It works well in place of rice in many recipes and everyone out here uses it a lot, since it will grow here.

We have large areas devoted to potatoes. Each place is growing all the potatoes we had left over from winter. With all the extra people, we will need all we can grow. They did bring a lot of food up with them and we have all shared around the different items they brought and shared what we had on hand.

When the weather gets cold enough for the meat to keep, we will butcher a couple of the cattle. They should be in good enough shape to give us a change of diet. For myself, anything but bear. I am so sick and tired of bear.

By the middle of the summer, the guys go check the river for fish. They have timed it well and bring back some large Kings. Tomorrow, they will start fishing in earnest to feed the dogs and anyone else that wants fish.

We soon have it set up like an assembly line processing the fish and getting them into the temporary smokehouse to dry. They bring the boat in loaded to the top with fish, we clean and hang them after slashing the sides to the skin. A smudge fire is kept going under the tarp covered walls, keeping the flies out and the smoke in. Soon we have bales of dried fish ready to store in everyone's storage sheds. The fish run is heavy and it doesn't take the men long to fill the boat. After one crew gets too tired to fish, another crew takes over. We are all working rotating shifts to keep it going as long as the run lasts.

When the fishing winds down, we have enough dried fish for all the dogs for the winter and a lot left over. The Kings were prepared as salmon strips for human consumption, the Silvers mostly for the dogs, just in case the chum don't run heavy enough later in the summer. Last year, they didn't run until the ice was forming and no one wanted to go out after them. The Silvers are okay for people to eat, also, if they want to. We take good care that they are all kept clean and not contaminated with dirt or fly blow. The guts are taken and buried in rows to be planted next year to squash and anything else needing a lot of fertilizer. No bears came in while we were taking care of fish, so no hams or bacon to fix this year, so far.

However, this year, we have turkeys. I butcher and clean a large tom and brine cure him to smoke. After he is cured, I smoke him in the smokehouse at home for a few days. Then I wrap and store in my ice house. This will be a surprise treat for Thanksgiving.

Elaine is not only walking all over the place, she is running all over the place and I have to keep her in a harness just to keep track of her. She is picking up words too, at the worst possible times. Shari's twins are talking a mile a minute. I don't always understand them, but they sure can understand each other. They seem to understand Elaine also.

Melanie had a little girl and she and Dan are spoiling her rotten already. That is certainly going to be a little princess that is in for some shocks in real life if they keep it up.

Al and Natalie are doing fine with their little boy. He is growing and a happy child. Farren looks after him as though he were the big brother and proud of everything he does. I enjoy visiting with them, not that we have time to visit much..

Progress on the 2 large houses is going well. Everyone tries to go help at least a couple of hours every day. We are also cutting extra firewood to fill their woodsheds as soon as they are built. It is being hauled over as we go to work and dumped near the site of the future woodsheds. The large barns are being framed in, as the houses are, since they are more important in some ways. There are places to the people to live, but not so for the animals.

Rose has some membrane roofing that is going to be used on most of the barn roofs at present. It isn't fireproof, but it is waterproof and available. None of us have the tools to weld or melt it on, but we can nail it on, then caulk over the nail heads.

It has been a fairly dry summer. So we keep watch for forest fires from any lightening strikes around. At least now, we don't have careless smokers or campers starting fires. We see distant plumes of smoke out across the valley below us, but that isn't too dangerous for us. Several rivers, swamp and lakes between those fires and us. If the wind changes, it can affect breathing and cloud the sun though.

Little things keep disappearing and everyone is noticing it. I just thought I was getting more forgetful until we started comparing notes. Then small items start showing up in place of what was taken. Someone was trying to trade for stuff without actually talking to any of us. A couple of plucked and cleaned grouse, wrapped in clean leaves, a tanned rabbit hide, things that could be used, but still, sometimes things that disappeared were things we wanted to keep. We did get better at putting stuff away. It has been going on all summer.

With everyone pitching in a few hours per day, we have most of the buildings watertight but not finished. We were now starting to cut hay. This year, we would really have to cut a lot. Everyone that had an old weed whacker, hand or motor, was out using them since most of the areas we cut were not accessible to cut with a tractor. Too steep or too rough. The tractor and mower are used along the roadbeds. We are certainly going to have to figure out better ways to handle this. We raked, gathered and stored as fast as it dried.

We would butcher more animals rather than let them go hungry, if we couldn't get enough hay stored.

The grain was growing well in the recently cleared areas, so everyone planned on helping harvest the heads of grain, just as soon as they started to ripen and were dry enough not to mold. I cut and hung bundles in my greenhouse and sun porch. My hay mow was as full as I could stuff it with dried hay, so I hung bundles of cut grain in the store room in the downstairs of the barn, also. When I ran out of room in those areas, I started hanging bundles inside the roof line of the woodsheds. I had to hang sheets over those to keep the birds out, though. As soon as the grain was dry, I beat the grains out of the bundles and put it in barrels in the storage rooms in the barn and woodshed.

Elaine learned some new words which she repeated to her Daddy tonight, when I dropped a barrel over on my foot. I don't think any bones are broken, but oh wow, that did hurt.

When her Grandpa comes over, the next day, she repeats them for him, also. He looked at us with narrowed eyes but doesn't say anything. I think he figured it out after I hobbled in to make some lunch for all of us. Dang, I am definitely going to have to watch my mouth no matter what, from now on.

The guys are making Earth Batteries for each new household. Galvanized rods and copper clad rods are driven 2 feet into the ground in a 2 foot grid, connected with electrical wire and checked with a muti-meter. One end of the wire is plus, the other end is negative. Adding more rods in sequence ups the amps after the volts is acquired. Not perfect, but we can use LED lights very well on them. A little light in the barns at night in the winter is really useful. For that matter, any light of any type in the winter is useful.

I think most of us are looking forward to some rest this coming winter. Summers are so short and so much work has to be done in order to survive the other months in some comfort. We have enough firewood for everyone, now. Some of the new places are building rocket mass heaters besides using the standard wood heaters. If the rocket heaters work as well for each household, it will simplify our wood cutting and save a lot of the trees.

The summer has been hot enough and dry enough that all the gardens are doing extremely well. We are harvesting and either canning or drying as much as possible. We can't count on every summer being this good. None of the springs have gone dry, so we continue to water the gardens and do laundry from them. I am using mine for drinking water and I think everyone else is also. I keep the tank by the house filled for showers all summer. All the ice containers are filled that we have used and in the ice house ready to be refroze this coming winter. We didn't run out until late August, this year.

Chapter 6

There is a fire somewhere in our valley. The smoke is too thick to tell exactly where or what size fire. I have to stay here with Elaine while Noah goes to check on it and see if the cattle and horse herd is okay, besides all our neighbors. I put as many of our animals as possible inside the barn and the chickens are closed up in their coop. If it isn't good for humans to breathe, it must not be good for them, either.

When he comes home that evening, he is exhausted and as black as coal. They found the fire and used the boat to haul people over across the river near the old bridge to fight it. The river is very small and the fire could jump it easily in several places. If the fire comes on across, it would be right in the herd and then all the places beyond Rose. The new area she opened up for growing grain and hay for the herd would be a good firebreak, but the grain is ripe and drying. They are also harvesting it as fast as they can, to see if they can back burn a bit on the straw and stop the fire if it gets that close.

Elaine and I go with him the next day. I stop at Will and Shari's and she offers to baby sit if I want to help on the harvesting that Rose, Liz and her daughters are doing while the men go fight the fire. I accept and walk on over to help out. They all have been out working on it since sunup. Shari sent over a large basket of food so they take a break and have something to eat.

The harvester they brought up in pieces from Delta has been assembled and is hooked up to one of the tractors. One has to ride on it to keep it filling the bin correctly as something seems to have been lost along the way. Another drives the tractor to pull it. When the bin is full, then back to the barn and dump the bin onto a large piece of the membrane roofing Rose had. Then back to fill the bin again.

While those 2 are gone, the rest of us fill bags, tie them and drag them into the barn to store on pallets until they figure out just where to put them. The other tractor is hooked to a mower and is cutting the straw close to the ground. Then after a large area is mowed, going back and raking it into windrows.

They have a small baler and then hook it up to bale the straw. By the end of the day, we have most of the grain stored in bags and most of the straw bales bucked onto the wagon and pulled into the barn. It isn't as important as the hay, but it will make fresh dry bedding for animals during the winter.

Since we managed to get it mostly all cut and baled, they won't have to burn it off to act as a firebreak. There really isn't much of anything left to burn.

By the time the fire crew comes back late in the evening, they are bone tired and so are we. I don't see Noah, so I ask each guy as they come by if they know whether he went on home or not. No one has any idea, they thought he was with someone else, as they are in small groups as they wander in.

Maybe he is so tired he forgot I came with him this morning. I go get Elaine and we head for home. She can walk most of the way herself now and it is a good thing. It has been too many years since I did any haying. I have aches where I didn't even know I had places.

Elaine and I grab a quick shower before going in the house and she is not thrilled with the cool water. I set her in one of the goat pens and milk the goat needing milked. Yes, I am letting a goat babysit and yes, I did think about letting her be raised by goats until she was old enough to housebroke, back when I first found out I was pregnant. I like to think I was only joking.

We take the fresh milk and go unlock the

front door. Noah isn't in the house, either. I take care of the milk and fix a meal for us. Then I take care of the chickens for the night. The turkeys are doing well and the hen raising some little turks looks funny perched up on top of them when they want to cuddle with mom.

Maybe Noah fell asleep over at his Dad's place. Elaine is about asleep but I bundle her back up and take my pickup over to find out.

Everyone is asleep at Roman's. I bang on the door until Thad stumbles over and opens it. He comes awake fast when I ask if Noah is there. No, he isn't. Thad comes with me as we go from house to house, asking about Noah.

Roman is dressed when we come back up the hill and he gets in the truck with us as we head back toward the fire. It isn't getting fully dark yet at night, so we go as close as possible with the pickup, then on foot. Thad carries Elaine as she has fallen asleep. We go where Noah was last seen by anyone, then follow the line he was cutting, clearing brush and trees. I see his boot first.

No, this is not happening. Roman tries to stop me but I am checking him out before they get entirely situated, with Elaine. She is still asleep. A tree has dropped it's top on him as he was cutting the bottom. It is called a Widow Maker with good reason. Today, it failed. He is still breathing and has a steady heartbeat.

I start pulling branches and parts of the tree away from him and Thad hands me my daughter. They find his chainsaw still in his hand and use it to cut the rest of the tree away.

By this time, the other folks we had woke up earlier are arriving to help. They make a litter and carefully lift and ease him onto the litter to carry him out. He is lifted into the back of my pickup and enough people are riding in back with him to hold the litter to keep it from jostling him around. Thad drives us to our home. Then he is carried inside and someone has brought in a flat piece of plywood to use as a backboard on the bed.

The litter is set carefully on the floor, first, so we can take off his boots, remove his sooty clothing and wash him a bit and try to find any injuries that we can repair while he is out. Once we have him fairly clean, the litter is again lifted and he is eased onto the board on the bed that is covered in an old piece of quilt from the supplies we brought from the Yukon Bridge trip.

It looks like he has a couple of broken ribs, which we can't do much for and a broken leg, which we will try to set before he comes to. Two of the guys hold his upper body and Roman gets a good hold on his foot and slowly eases the leg out straight. It pops and appears to be okay, just dislocated. We can't tell anything much about his back, neck or head so we wrap him up as well as we can without moving his back or neck, then cover him and hope he wakes up in the morning. Everyone is completely wiped out by the days work and now half the evening finding Noah and bringing him home. Roman tells me to stay home tomorrow, they have it covered.

I awake to Noah muttering in his sleep. I am sleeping on a pile of sofa cushions on the floor by the bed so I wouldn't bump him. He is flailing around, with his arms, so I grab his hand and start talking to him. He quietens as soon as I touch him and start talking, so I pull my cushions over and settle in for a long night.

In the morning, I must have finally dozed off, because I wake up to him rubbing my head and muttering again. Sitting in a pile of cushions with your head against a bed isn't the most comfortable nights sleep, but I had to feel better than he did.

Rose came over a little later. She brought some essential oils to put on his leg and ribs and some herbs to make tea to sooth him a bit, once he wakes up. She said it would probably do me some good, too. He was badly bruised, so she put some lavender and cypress oils on him besides the wintergreen

and peppermint. She said she was really
going to miss them when she ran out finally. I
knew she was worried about Noah since she
was using the oils full strength instead of
diluting them as she usually did for other
hurts and pains. We rewrap his scrapes and
scratches and he appears to be sleeping more
restfully. She apologizes for not coming right
over last night, but no one let her know what
had happened. She says she will come back
over tonight to check on him again and redo
the oils. She asks if I have cayenne. I do, so
she tells me to make some cayenne capsules
to give him to stop any internal bleeding,
once he is conscious. She gives me a baggie
of gelatin capsules to make up for him.

About an hour after she left, he wakes up. I
ask him to wiggle toes and fingers and feet
and knees. He looks at me funny but does it.
Then he raises one leg, then the other. I
think his back is okay.

I help him scoot over to the other side of
the bed and remove the plywood. He has no
memory of getting hurt. I make up a cayenne
capsule and give it to him with some of the
tea Rose left. He is very sore all over and
wants to now if I beat him with a bat while he
slept. I tell him as much as we figured out
and how he got home.

He wants to get up and go back to work.
We have a small disagreement about that until

he tries to get up. Then he agrees he might need a couple of days off. Elaine is so happy to have Daddy at home during the day that she keeps him entertained while I go take care of chores.

He insists on getting up to eat dinner that night. So I help him stumble his painful way to the table. He is sweating and pale by the time we get there.

By the time we are done eating, he looks better but still not all that great. His Dad and brother come over with Rose to doctor him. They help him back to bed, scolding all the way. Rose oils his bruises and leg, then some on the lump on the back of his head we couldn't do while he was unconscious. He gets another cayenne capsule and more soothing tea.

She suggests I continue twice a day at least on the capsules for a week. Then if he has any internal bleeding, it should be stopped and healed up some. But to watch his abdomen for any tightness, distension or bruised look. He should check his stools for any signs of blood, also. Anything at all, start on the cayenne again.

He will have to be careful with his ribs so he doesn't puncture a lung or his heart. As he listened to this, he looked a bit more pale. After they leave, he asks me if he had been in danger. I tell him of course he was, he almost died. If he wasn't careful now until he healed up some, he still could.

He didn't argue the next morning when I brought him breakfast in bed. Elaine thought it was a new game and wanted hers in bed with Daddy.   After doing the morning chores, I worked in the garden to get caught up on weeding and harvesting.

The greenhouse is a jungle. I pick and take armloads of produce into the house. Noah is reading to Elaine, so I get as much done as I can before he wears out or she gets tired of being so still. The novelty of having Daddy to herself is lasting far longer than I expected and when I go in later, they are both asleep, curled up on the bed.

The potatoes have died back, so I dig on them a while. This is going to take a few days, I planted a very large potato patch this year.

The barn cat that we found in Fairbanks after the earthquake is doing a great job keeping the voles down. There is almost no damage to the potatoes. I hate leaving her outside, but she is so afraid of buildings I can't get her in the house. She likes the barn since it is usually open and other animals in it. We keep a fire going in it in the coldest weather, so she seems to do okay. She lost most of her ears before we found her, from freezing and part of her tail and paw pads.

By the time I finish up and rinse off before coming in, they are awake and he is trying to keep her entertained in the bedroom. She is usually very active and I am surprised she is doing as well as she is. I fix dinner and we all eat in the bedroom tonight.

The next morning, Elaine is awake before Noah, so I take her out and run her around the yard to tire her out before leaving her with him most of the day. It works for me, for her? Not so much.

We wash off and go in to cook breakfast and find Noah already up and trying to do it himself. The effort has him sweating and not looking so good, but breakfast is ready. We eat and he barely makes it back to the bedroom before collapsing on the bed. When Rose and Roman get there, he is looking pretty bad and has a bit of fever. She is quietly bawling him out all the time she is doctoring him. I think he will stay in bed for a few more days before trying that again.

By afternoon, his fever has risen and I am getting worried. I sponge him off with cool water which he fights. I make some willow tea which I get spooned down him, then sponge him off some more. Some of his bruising seems to have enlarged in area, so the cayenne gets increased. Now every time he is lucid and awake, he is getting another capsule of it. I even add some to the tea I keep having him sip on.

When Roman and Rose come back over that evening, she is worried and then Roman is, also. I have been all day. They wrap a larger area of his torso with compression bandages. Then, when they leave, she tells me they are going down and have Richard come over and see what he suggests and Thad will be over to spend the night. I don't even argue.

When Thad and Richard get there, Noah is awake but not looking good. They bring in some pieces of wood to put under the head of the bed legs and raise his head a bit. He is not breathing very well and pneumonia is always a possibility. Richard has him deep breathe and tells him he has to do that several times a day, no matter how much it hurts his ribs.

The men have been doing mop up work on the fire, but it seems to have petered out pretty much at the fire line they cut and the river. A windblown spark started another small fire but one of the kids saw it start and they quickly got it put out. The sudden rain shower that hit later that night pretty much finished it.

Chapter 7

Noah is not a very good patient. Although the onset of the fever and weakness did scare him into staying in bed for several days. Thad and Roman took turns coming over to spend the night helping keep an eye on him. I knew they had a lot to do at home to get ready for winter, yet, so tried to make sure they didn't spend too much time here.

That made Noah feel guilty and he wanted to get up again. I finally told him he was going to cause a lot more problems for all of us if we had to keep checking to see if he was following orders to stay in bed. We had too much to do to babysit him as well as Elaine. Her, I could put in the puppy pen or with the baby goats and she stayed happy and played without complaint. I hated to think what all went into her mouth, but she was thriving and happy.

She saw enough other people not to be totally afraid of strangers and I never thought to try to make her leery of any, since we didn't get strangers around here, now. So the day she was out of the goat pen and I had to hunt for her, only to find her out near the main road with a flower with a piece of leather tied to it, scared me half to death. When she said the big man gave it to her, I about passed out. Then she handed it to me and said, "For you, Mommy." I just sat on the ground and hugged her to me. What was happening to our family?

I couldn't tell Noah. He had enough problems right now without worrying about us and his not being able to take care of us. I told Roman, Thad and Rose. They would pass the word on to everyone and maybe someone would find out who was hanging around.

Jeremy stopped over to see Noah and when he came outside to leave, he asked if he could check around my place and see if he could find any clues or set up some means of finding out who it had been. Having been Special Forces, he knew a lot of things the rest of us didn't.

When he came back to the house a couple of hours later, he said he found an area where it looked like someone was keeping the house under surveillance. He had some supplies he picked up from the marauder camp we took out a couple of winters ago and would set a trap for the guy. He was going to catch this guy. I don't ask for specifics.

A few days later, he stops by to visit Noah again and as he is leaving, he says, "Problem solved." and leaves.

Okay, what happened? Hey, I would like a little bit more information here, well, after thinking it over, maybe I don't. Jeremy is a really nice guy but sometimes his skills are a bit scary.

I quit misplacing things or getting unwanted trades after that, so I guess whoever it was has been watching for quite a while.

Noah is slowly improving and it is about time as far as his nerves and my patience is going. I know it is hard on him not to be able to do stuff, but to listen to him grousing around about it doesn't help at all. I guess this is the "In sickness and in health" part of our marriage vows and I need to keep remembering that. Just about the time I am ready to explode, he looks at me with his lovely eyes and tells me how much he loves me, and wow, I turn to mush. I think maybe I have been wallowing in self pity a little bit, okay, quite a bit.

Chapter 8

Our August rains have set in and are making up for lost time. Everyone is hurrying on finishing the inside of the cabins and houses framed in earlier this summer for all the new members of our community.

Noah still has to take it easy, but he can walk now without passing out which is always a step forward in recovery. We walk a lot to help him get his strength back and rebuild muscle lost from enforced bed rest. So one day we find ourselves at Liz's place and go in and help them insulate. They have already finished the upstairs insulation, foam board and vapor barrier. Elaine is happy to play with the wrappers and we caulk all the electrical outlets and the tubing for propane lights where they come through the walls. By the time we head home, Noah is feeling very tired, so we stop and visit a while with his Dad.

When he feels better, we head on home. He takes Elaine in the house to start dinner and I go milk and feed the animals. Life seems to be getting back to normal and I like it. I don't like the types of surprises we have been getting, lately.

At least I can relax a bit, with the garden and greenhouse. The garden is mostly harvested and the greenhouse is still producing quite well. If frost holds off, I should have enough ripe tomatoes to can some. We are keeping a small fire going in the greenhouse to help keep it producing longer. I have the late started leaf lettuce transplanted and on the sun porch already and some of the 5 gallon buckets with tomato plants are on the porch, also, for fresh tomatoes at least until Christmas. Several of the herbs are now in pots on the sun porch to have fresh herbs for cooking most of the winter.

The first morning we have a bit of frost, I start up the generator and do all the laundry we have on hand and redo most of our bedding to have fresh during the winter. Then I drain the water tanks and put the washer away for another winter. I top off all the water containers in the house and on the porch. Back on our winter schedule for water.

We have placed the largest propane tank we brought from the Yukon River back between the house and the ice house and hooked lines up to both. All the smaller tanks are stored in the small room in the woodshed out of sight.

If we use it carefully only for cooking and a light or two in winter, it should last us several years. When I used the 300 gallon tank on just the stove and a light, it would last 3 years and this is a much larger tank.

We have made a small shed around this large tank and it looks like another old storage shed if not checked too closely. There is no reason for anyone to see it. I don't want anyone getting jealous of what we have and trying to take it from us. There has been enough killing without adding petty jealousy as a reason for more.

The men have started construction down by the river, of a fish wheel. Sooner or later, we are going to run out of gas that will run the boat as well as it does now. So while the boat is still working, they are going to build a fish wheel and make sure they have it right, before they truly need it. Our little river is a clear water stream, so it isn't going to work very well unless it spans the whole river or we build wings out to funnel the fish into it. I think the wings idea is what they will go for.

By the time they have it done, it is freezing every night. So everyone harvests the last from the greenhouses and gardens and prepares for the snow that can't be too far behind the frosts.

Steve and Dani come by to visit and show us Boy 2. Boy 1 has grown a lot and is a fine little guy. They are still just going to let the boys choose their own names when they get older. They let us know how the cattle and horses taken farther north are doing and that everyone has cut hay and have shelters built for them. Next spring, they plan on taking some on over to Manley and setting them up to farm a bit, too. They head home soon after lunch. Travel isn't all that easy now.

The first snowfall isn't bad, so everyone goes and helps round up the cattle out of the deadfall fenced area near the river and bring them up to the grain fields we harvested during the fire. The horses are kept in the field on one side of the creek and the cattle are put on the other.

We check our traps and snares and plan on using some of the butcher scraps as bait. A day is planned for butchering and they have chosen the 2 steers they want butchered. They were placed in another pen far away from the main herd and out of sight of it. We take our pickup over, the day they butcher and help as much as possible. We will use the gut pile as a bait for wolves, later.

While we are there, it is mentioned that Mike needs a shop to work in, in the winter. They have an area leveled and a gravel pad placed and settled. So everyone is going to come over in the next few days and build a shop. He is surprised it is going to be a group effort.

We built Romans' cabin in 2 days, we should be able to build a shop the same way. He managed to build himself a sawmill this summer and has boards cut to side it. We will use logs as post and beam construction and it goes fairly fast with as many willing hands as we have, helping.

There is a good lunch waiting when a break is called at noon. Shari has Elaine, so I am not worried. They love having her there and she loves them, too. I really like Mike's family and we work side by side putting up boards on the sides as the frame is completed. We get acquainted as we work and I invite them to come visit any time.

By the time we quit for the day, it is getting late and we should have milked an hour ago. I am so glad we have the pickup today. I don't think I could have made it walking home and carrying Elaine. I think Noah has overdone it, also. He says he hasn't, but he is really happy to get home and relax a bit. I offer to do the goats and chickens if he will take care of Elaine and start dinner. About the time we head for our chores, there is lights coming in our driveway, so we wait and see who it is. When we recognize Roman's pickup, we put the guns down and meet him. He says we took off too fast, they had dinners prepared for everyone to take home since we all worked all day and he brought ours. Okay, Noah gets the easy chores tonight.

I hurry up with the milking while Noah and his Dad visit. Then we eat dinner. It is delicious, but then, it has been a while since we have had someone else fix our dinner for us. Noah washes up the dishes and Roman takes them with him when he leaves to return them tomorrow.

I gather eggs and put out fresh feed and water, but the chickens are already bedded down and grumble as I work.

By the time I get back in the house, Elaine is asleep in her bed and Noah is getting ready for bed, also. I'm not sure I can get my boots off, even. It has been a while since I was this tired.

The morning is clear and cold, but not snowing, so we go back to work on the shop. We are a little late showing up as we overslept. That's our story and we are sticking to it.

By late afternoon, the shop is weather tight. The roof is on and the walls are up. He just has doors and windows to place and hook up a stove, then if he has any type of insulation, start insulating the inside. For this winter, he is going to use straw bales.

Chapter 9

We go home and relax in front of the fire
we stoked up as soon as we walked in the
door. Ahhh, it feels good to relax with
nothing needing done right this minute to
make us feel guilty.

Before dark, we do the outside chores and
refill the indoor wood box. Since we are
caught up on things around here, we are
going to see how a rocket mass heater is to
build. We will do the initial burner and pipe
outdoors to see if our layout will draw before
attempting it in the house.

The next day, we assemble all the supplies
we have gathered for this project. We build a
frame of the firebrick I had in my salvage
shed. Then we put a 5 gallon bucket with
both ends cut out as a wood feed. Then
another one with one end open turned upside
down over the firebrick burner area. Then a
55 gallon barrel with one end cut out is
upended over that 5 gallon bucket as a smoke
chamber to redirect the smoke back down to
the pipe that is going out a hole cut in the
lower edge of the upended barrel. It makes

sense when you see a picture.

The pipe needs a cleanout at each turn, so we find all our pipe and pipe supplies to make sure we have enough for what we have planned. Once we lay it out on the ground, we build a small fire in the fire box and stick small branches down the feeder bucket. It burns pretty well although our feeder bucket may be too large. So we measure the whole works and then go in and measure and move stuff in the living room to make room to build it. Then we put metal sheets down where we want to place the heater with pieces of sheetrock under the metal. We bend the edges of the metal up for a lip all the way around it, then place flat stones on top of the metal.

The fire has died down in the firebox, so we disassemble it all and take the pieces in the house. We lay it all out again, and find where we need to place the outside chimney in our wall. We place more stones around the pipe and firebox sections. Then we fill in around them with gravel. Then we start mixing the COB mess in a large open water tank we use for the goats outside in summer. This is where it gets messy.

We brought several bales of the straw home from Liz's place and we need to chop it up and mix it with the clay and sand. The sand is coarse river sand, not fine beach sand, so not sure how it is going to work. I try stomping the mixture in my rubber boots but it sucks them right off. So we fix a bucket of warm water to use later to clean my feet and legs and I just hop in barefoot. I'm wearing a pair of old holey cut off jeans that I used the legs to make pants for Elaine out of, when someone knocks on the door.

Noah answers the door and puts the gun down behind the door as he opens it to let our visitors in. Could I be more embarrassed, well, yes I could. I was just going to do it naked. It is Al and Natalie with their little boy, Walter, and Farren. I continue stomping as we talk until the mixture seems to be well mixed and the right consistency to place over what we have constructed.

They are interested in what we are doing and soon after I clean up my feet and legs in the bucket, we are all using our hands to place the muck over the framework on the floor. Elaine and Walter join in and are getting as much on them as on the framework. Farren helps out and is excellent at spotting areas we have missed.

Natalie sits on the floor chuckling and says she will have to come visit more often, she never knows what to expect when she gets here, but always enjoys it. By the time we run out of the mud, it is getting late afternoon and I have a pot of stew on the stove, all I have to do is add milk to the dumpling batter I have ready. So I mix and drop them in as we talk, after I clean up a bit. The guys and Natalie are cleaning up the little ones while I fix our meal. I have some sticky buns I used birch syrup to make and we will have those for dessert, unless we decide to eat them while the dumplings cook.

That sounds best to everyone and we start on dessert first. Our first batch of ice cream is frozen on the porch, so we bring that in to share with the buns. By the time the dumplings are done, we are not very hungry, but we manage to eat a good portion of it anyway.

As they are getting ready to leave, Al says all the turkey eggs I gave them hatched and survived so they have too many turkeys. They want to know if we want one for our holiday meal. They plan on keeping a pair alive with their chickens but can't winter over the rest. He wants to butcher in the next few days so they don't suffer from being out in the cold and snow. He thinks one a month during the winter is about all the roast turkey he wants to eat plus the soup afterwards for a couple of days with each turkey.

The next morning, we start another batch of mud to work on our heater. We are shaping it in an L pattern with the firebox in the middle and each leg a couch of sorts.

The pipe goes through both legs of the L. We cut the hole through the wall and put a section of insulated pipe through then put a cap over it. There is supposed to be very little heat lost out the pipe but we use insulated pipe anyway. Today is almost a repeat of yesterday. I stomp mud and straw and sand, Noah, Elaine and I slap it on the form we are making. We are making it a freeform couch with room to sleep on it if we feel like it. We have the 55 gallon barrel almost completely enclosed in the mud. We are leaving the top end of it open to radiate more heat and to cook on or heat water on. The whole thing is placed about a foot from the outside walls. We want as much air circulation around it as possible.

The dry air in the house and the heat from our heater are drying the mud fairly fast, so it does crack a bit here and there. We fill the cracks as they show up with more mud. We put the burner facing the center of the room, right in front, so no one on the couches would be apt to drop something in it or get burned by it. We needed to make some sort of metal lid to keep Elaine from feeding it her toys or getting burned by accident. We finally added a metal frame around it that she couldn't reach through but we could unhook and fuel it up.

This time the knock on the door wasn't

until we were getting cleaned up a bit from our mudding. Again, Noah answered as I went into our bedroom to add a real pair of pants instead of the holey shorts. This time it was his Dad and Rose. We hadn't even heard them drive up, we were so engrossed in what we were doing. Then they told us to go see what they were driving.

Roman has made a pony cart and he is keeping one of the mares Liz brought up. Instead of a regular horse harness, he made a combo harness that looked more like a giant dog harness. It just slipped over her head and then a bridle with very long reins was used to guide her with. The reins slipped through a loop in the middle of the horses' back on the harness. Looked odd, worked well. He was going to build one for Liz, next.

Wow, now I might have to rethink not getting a horse. This could be fun and a horse can do a lot of work besides just for riding. Now that we needed to hay and grow grain, a horse would be a lot of help on the planting and harvesting part. Of course, they would eat a lot of it, too. I will wait and see how it goes for everyone else, I think.

They have brought some lemon cake with the pudding between layers and we still have some ice cream, so we eat dessert again tonight. Usually, Noah and I only have dessert once a week to stretch the sugar we have as many years as possible. We do use the birch syrup instead whenever we can to sweeten with. It makes good ice cream.

They look over our creation of a heater and ask when we are going to fire it up. We are thinking we might as well right now to see if it draws indoors as well as it did, outdoors. It does, yay. We even have witnesses. This would have been a real pain to have to tear it all apart and take it out. Besides, as much as I like house work, it would probably stay right where it is, working or not, until at least next year. Or the year after.....

When we fire it up, the barrel top starts radiating heat almost immediately. The rest will have to warm up and as damp as the mixture we slapped on it is, that is going to take some drying time as well as just warming up the whole mass. I can see it will take it a long time to cool off once it is all warm. I'm not sure it will heat the whole house though and the chickens out in the coop against the sun porch. We will see.

Rose and I look our work in progress over and she suggests adding in a shelf/oven arrangement in the area against the barrel but facing the front, over the firebox.

We start removing some of the mud we plastered over the area, before it gets baked too hard. Roman says he has a metal box with a hinged lid that he will bring over tomorrow for us to place in there and maybe a couple of other items that will make it even better.

After they leave, we clean up the mess a bit and put all the scraps of muck and clay back in the tank. We will need to mix more tomorrow.

The next morning, Roman is back with some pieces of metal and a nice metal box. It nearly fits perfectly in the opening we made in the COB last night. We situate it in place and level it. Then we start adding more COB around it to hold it in place. We brace it with a board until the COB is dry enough to support it in place. We keep building small fires in it to speed up the drying.

Since this seems to be working, we decide to try it next year in a greenhouse and build the planting beds on the areas that will be the couches here in the house. It might be easier to build it then move the greenhouse over it. Not something we can do now since it is below freezing but we can start making plans and rounding up supplies.

We spend most of the next week tweaking and filling small cracks in the COB as it dries. Elaine has so much fun with it, that we hate to finish the project. So I make her some play dough to keep her busy. She doesn't like the taste of it any better than the COB so it stays out of her mouth.

Chapter 10

We have enough snow now, to hitch up the dogs and make some runs with the sled. When the dogs see the harnesses come out and the sled, they are so excited they are bouncing at the ends of their chains. We finally get a team hooked up and Elaine all bundled up and make a trip up to see Al and Natalie.

We aren't really stopping to visit, just giving the dogs some harness time and starting the trails for winter. We talk a few minutes outdoors where they are working on finishing stacking firewood in the shed. Then we turn and make a run to see Roman and Thad.

They have been clearing out the yard around their cabin and have a nice turn around shoveled out. The dogs hit it at full speed and make the circle a couple of times just for the fun of it. Elaine is laughing and enjoying herself very much. Their dogs out back are excited and yelping up a storm. We finally got stopped and Roman and Thad came out of the shop. One of the young men living over near Kara came out with them. He wants to learn how to do wood work like they do, so they are teaching him. I hope we get some of their projects headed our way, they always make such interesting items.

When we return home, we make the team run beside our first trail to widen the trail for the winter. They want to run in the first trail so they don't have to break trail, so we aren't as successful as we had hoped to be.

The pups left behind are jumping around like crazy when we return to the house. We change out the team and put the one we are hoping will be a new leader in the lead and the others in line behind him. Then Noah takes them for a circle around the yard and out the driveway. They are so excited he has a hard time turning them around to come back after a short run. We prefer to keep them excited about pulling, so they don't dread getting hooked up. After they are back on their chains, we snack them all with a dried fish as a treat for a job well done.

While they howl their evening chorus, we hear an answering howl from across the valley. Then several more join in and our bunch shut right up. It sounds like a large pack of wolves moving into our area. This is not good news for our outdoor animals.

When we get up the next morning, we put the barbed wire electric fence back up around the perimeter of the yard. The team and the barn are inside it, so maybe it will deter any wolves from coming on it. We will have to make sure everyone is watching out for their animals. A domestic horse or cow in a field is a lot easier to pull down than a wild moose or caribou that is used to running on snow. A few years ago, a pack of wolves dragged a young boy away from one of the villages downriver. There have been other attacks also, but usually not well advertised. The lady jogger on the Alaska Peninsula that was killed and eaten by wolves is not widely known about, either. She was wearing her headphones and probably never knew what hit her.

I did not want my animals or family to be their next meal. So I make sure I had plenty of snares ready to set and placed some in trails leading into our yard. It is too early for the fur to be prime, but we would use it, if we get any. We drag out the frozen gut pile from the butchering earlier this month and take it out where we used to have the bear gut pile. I reset snares all around the outer perimeter and place sticks in the other trails to deter them from using trails with no snares on them.

We can spot the snares from a distance with

the binoculars we carry for just that purpose. That way, we don't have to get too close and scent up the area to check the snares. We check morning and evening and about a week later, when we go out in the morning to check, the ground is all torn up around the gut pile and we head over to check. We have 5 wolves in snares. We load them on the sled and clean up the area around the bait. We will probably never catch another wolf from that pack in a snare if any survived. They will be very cautious after this.

We are thawing and skinning the wolves when Roman and Rose come over. Rose helps me skin while the guys discuss something in the kitchen. They might as well have stayed in here, Rose tells me what they are talking about and Noah would anyway, after they left.

Jeremy has seen signs of some people sneaking around all the places out here. He thinks they came across the valley after the rivers froze over, instead of from town or farther north.

Finally the guys give up and come in and we all talk it over. I was hoping all the people not willing to work for their food were long gone. They have managed to steal one of the young cows out of the field at Liz and Richard's and butchered it just out of sight of the house. They didn't even salvage all the meat, they just took some and left the rest. So they were wasteful as well as thieves.

Our electric fence would help us hear if anyone came sneaking into our yard, but no one else had that type of set up. My snares might help us out, also.

Jeremy was going to see about tracking them and finding where they were camping and we would pay them a visit.

The next night, Jeremy stopped by and told us he tracked them back across the river toward the south. They may be going for reinforcements.

Early the next morning, Jeremy, Thad and Dan took off in Dan's plane to see if they could find them. They spotted them huddled under some small trees and Jeremy opened the side window and dropped some of the grenades he found in the marauders camp we had demolished a couple of years ago. The results were gory. Dan landed on the ice a short distance away, and the men went over to see what or who they had found.

The first person Dan saw was Amy. "Looks like I should have dropped you off without landing a few years ago, Amy. Did you decide you still didn't have to work for what you wanted?"

She pulled a handgun out of her coat and aimed it at Dan's head. "Well, at least now I get to take you with me."

Jeremy appeared right behind her and before she could pull the trigger, he knocked her arm down and twisted it behind her back. She turned on him and started to hit him, he twisted a bit more and her arm snapped. She fainted and he removed the gun from her reach and checked for more weapons.

The rest of the bunch with her were dead but looked like they were in very good physical condition, so either they were very good at stealing or they were just easy keepers. They were soon stripped of any clothing that could be used and their packs loaded into the plane. They had most of the choice cuts taken from the cow they had butchered still in their packs and on the sled they were pulling.

"Okay, now what do we do with her? If we just leave her here, is she going to show up again with another group of thieves? She has a broken arm and some major cuts and possibly a broken leg. Do you want to take her home?"

Nobody wanted to take her home, least of all, Thad. When he and Al found her and Natalie, she tried clinging onto Thad as hers. He didn't want her. Then she started making trouble for everyone else. Finally, she was flown near a small community to the south and dropped off with bags of food.

"Say, do you suppose that tractor trailer unit

is still along the road? We aren't all that far from it. Let's leave her here and think about it while we check that out and stop on our way back after we decide."

Sounds like a plan, so they get back in the plane and took off to check out the tractor trailer they had found after dropping her off a couple of years ago.

They find the tractor trailer unit and it appears to have not been touched since their last visit. It is on a sharp curve and evidently foot traffic has been taking a short cut across the curve and never seen it at all.

Dan lands and they brush snow off the doors then open them. The trailer is still in great shape and the flour and sugar appear fine. They load as much as they can manage to stuff into the plane and reclose the doors. Now the sled and packs they picked up from the thieves was strapped to the top of the plane.

They take a lot farther to take off than they did on the ice on the river. They are vastly overloaded.

As they near the area where they left Amy, they see movement around the area. A very large black bear is feeding on the remains of Amy. It is too bad about Amy, but she choose the way she wanted to live. That was probably not her choice on how to die, but her choices landed her there.   The men are very quiet all the way home.

When the men get home, they are very subdued and it is a while before they tell us what happened. It's not like they led the bear over and said, here, stock up before winter hits any harder and you den up. I might have done that, but the guys didn't.

So now we get to wonder and worry whether Amy was with a larger group and this was only a small scouting party or what. Even though no sign of any camp was seen from the air, that doesn't mean there isn't more waiting to hear from this bunch back in the community she had been dropped off near. She had been good at insinuating herself into other people's lives and playing them to her own ends.

The flour and sugar are great additions to everyone's supply. With it being frozen over half of each year, it stays fresh longer than flour stored in a home heated year around. We put ours in totes out in the ice house. Might as well keep it as cold as possible year around.

After delivering flour and sugar along the road, Dan fuels the plane back up at the fuel truck before parking it again.

We are all very careful not to use too much of the fuel from any of the trucks brought down from the Yukon River Bridge. We will probably never have another supply once it is gone. Before the large propane tank Liz and Richard brought from Canada is hooked up to their house and still in the front bucket of the large tractor, they bring it to the propane truck and top it off. We give the smaller of the 2 propane tanks we got at the Yukon to Mike and his family for their house. They cook on wood, but it is handy for lights and will last them for years used only for that.

Since we now have a lot more flour than I ever expected to have on hand again, I make a huge batch of potato doughnuts to share around the community. Even though I have a lot of flour on hand, I still mix other grain flour in with the wheat flour to extend it farther.

While I am frying them, Al, Natalie and family show up, so I send their share home with them. Then Roman drops by and I send enough for him to dole out all around their area. Noah comes in from seeing his Dad off, and grabs a couple still hot from the pan. Poor dear, he didn't think he was going to get any. Then I hand him one of the ones I made as bars and filled with pudding. He is savoring it when I whisper in his ear and the doughnut is left on the counter as we race for the bedroom, to be pulled up short by another knock on the door. I swear, make doughnuts or bake bread and people can smell it for miles around.

Noah yells out, "Who is it?" Still tugging me toward the bedroom.

"Steve, from up the road."

"Okay, just a minute."

He grabs the gun by the door, just in case, and opens the door to find Steve, Dani and Boys 1 and 2. He puts the gun back as they come in. I set out a plate of still warm doughnuts and they soon have their mouths full. I have more to fry and keep turning out doughnuts.

Everyone is finally filled up and we have a nice visit. We have the wolf pelts drying on stretchers near the porch door and Steve looks them over. For early pelts, they are in pretty good shape. I think I will make a parka for Noah with them. Between what I have on hand and these, I should be able to match enough furs to make it look good. I will use the faces to make Trapper hats or mitts.

We are still working on our mass heater and it is starting to work pretty good. We show Steve and Dani how it works. They are interested in making one for the new house they want to build since their little cabin is getting crowded.

After they leave, Noah looks at me and asks where we were, when interrupted. Then Elaine wails from the bedroom and that ends that for a while.

Chapter 11

Al brings us a turkey, already butchered, cleaned and frozen. He remembers how I am about animals and birds I have raised. This helps a lot, as I still can't bring myself to kill the ones I have cuddled and held. When I hunt, I have to set my mind to look at the animals as steaks, roasts and burger and then shoot as soon as I see a legal one. If I take the time to look at them and appreciate how magnificent they are, then I can't shoot them. The same with birds even. Anything that is threatening me or my family is a different story altogether.

Somehow, we ended up with a very late kid goat. So now I worry she will freeze to death as she is a very tiny little thing. I make a blanket for her with a hood of sorts to go over part of her head. I figure if people lose so much body heat from their head, animals probably do also. I rub the whole thing over the baby and her mother to get their scent on the outside of it before lacing her into it. The mother is suspicious but accepts her. Now we have to keep the fire going earlier than usual in the barn. The little LED lights give some light all day in there for the animals so they aren't shut away in the dark all the time. We have some straw from the grain harvest at Liz and Richard's so they have clean dry beds.

About the time I think I have that little one all fixed up, Liz shows up with a small heifer calf that the mother won't accept. This is definitely not the time of year for calves to be born up here. So I put the other blanket I made a couple of years ago for a larger kid goat on the calf and stick her in with the kid goat. It won't fit her long and I will have to make a bigger one. I milk out some of the colostrum from the goat and give it to the calf. The goat sniffs her and accepts her so I won't have to do that again. But I don't want her nursing too much and will have to find an alternate means of feeding her. Probably let her suck my fingers as I lower them into a bucket of milk.

The calf is very small, so the first week is mostly just keeping her alive. We keep the fire going 24/7 in the barn for her and the kid goat. Since I check on them often, I start them both on halter training and being handled a lot. They think they are sisters and both play and buck around in their little pen near the stove. They sleep in a pile of straw, closest to the stove, cuddled together.

With their little hooded blankets, they look like little elves. They shiver when I take the blankets off, so I hurry and put the larger ones I have made on them. Poor babies, they are still very small and winter isn't very warm. By the end of October, it is staying near 20 below zero F.

One morning as I am pitching hay down into the hay rack below me, I hear a definite "Ow" from the pile I am jabbing the pitchfork into. Oops, now what?

I pull hay back more carefully and there is a young girl down in the hay. She has a black eye and a bruised cheek. She ducks back when I reach down to help her out of the hay. "Come on, I'm not going to smack you unless you take a swing at me first."

She finally comes out of the hay, brushing herself off as well as she can. She shows signs of having minor frostnip but not a lot, so she hasn't come far dressed as she is, in this weather. We go in the house and Noah is very surprised to see someone show up without the dogs letting us know.

She is very thin, so we fix a good breakfast and she isn't picky, she eats everything. After breakfast, she is hesitant to talk much. She shies away any time someone moves very fast, so I am thinking she has been smacked a lot before the current black eye and bruised cheek.

She says she is 18, and don't want to live at home any more. She also says she has a parka in the barn, getting dried out behind the stove as she was running a lot to get here and it got damp with sweat. She says she is from the other side of the small community to the north of us, and she was afraid her step dad would search for her there. She overheard Dani talking about us one time and decided she could make it here, instead. So she is a lot tougher than she looks. She has probably traveled close to 40 miles on foot in fairly cold weather.

We concentrate on getting her full. The girl is a bottomless pit when it comes to food. She doesn't eat huge quantities at one time, but can and does eat every time food is mentioned. She finally manages to tell us her name is Annie.

I go back out and get her parka and bring it in. If her step dad comes around, I don't want evidence hanging out in plain sight. She says she walked on down to the other driveway and mingled her tracks in with all the other foot traffic there, before coming back here late last night.

The moon was bright, so she saw the fence, didn't realize it was electric, and almost yelled when it bit her. But she had a lot of practice staying quiet, so she didn't make a sound and went on into the barn. She said animals like her, so she just kept talking low and gentle and none of them made any noise. She stoked up the fire and climbed up in the loft and dug down to keep warm and went to sleep. I barely grazed her leg with the pitchfork and we dressed it after cleaning it out.

The next morning, the dogs set up a howling and we check out the windows. There is a team coming in our drive. Annie knows the driver and one of his two companions and turns pale. It is her step dad and his buddies. I send her to our bedroom and mostly close the door. Elaine is sleeping in the room beyond.

The man pounds on the door demanding entrance, so Noah takes his time about answering. I am at my side window with the shotgun full of slugs. As Noah opens the door, I open the window a little bit. When the man starts to shove Noah back, I cock the hammer and suggest he not do that. The man starts blustering about us not being very neighborly. Well, you know? If you come to my door with an attitude, then you are going to be met with an attitude.

We let them come in, but I sit there with the shotgun in my hands the entire time. I have shut my window. The man starts to get demanding and I ease back on the hammer again and suggest a better attitude might help.

He is about to blow a gasket, he looks like a stroke about to happen. I didn't know anyone could get that red in the face and look like they puffed up 2 or 3 sizes. I'm thinking his buddies have never seen anyone stand up to this man. They don't know whether to giggle or be shocked. Shock wins out.

"Now, what is so important that you try to pound my door down?" Noah asks.

The man starts two or three times and finally picks a story to tell us. His poor little daughter is lost and they are searching for her to take her home. She is supposed to be getting married next week to Jake, here, the grinning goon. The other one looks surprised.

The man stinks and is at least twice her age. He might have 2 or 3 teeth and looks like he lost a fight with a bear at some time from the scar tissue all over his face and arms. I ask and he mumbles no, he just lost a fight to their exalted leader here, Rhyse. After he lost, Rhyse held his face against the wood heater and burned him to show him who was boss. His arms got burned trying to push away from the stove. The girl was his, she was promised to him for work he did for Rhyse.

"Did she agree to this?" I ask.

"Heck no, she didn't know until 2 days ago."

Noah tells them we will let her know they are looking for her, if she shows up here.

Jake tugs on Rhyse's sleeve, trying to get his attention and whining they should search the place.

I kinda let the shotgun wander in his direction and gently suggest that would not be such a good idea. He turns pale and agrees. They leave and we watch them out of sight. The girl comes out of our bedroom and says they will sneak back around and come in behind us now.

We ask her to stay in the house and we gear up and head out to the driveway to see which direction they will come from. They have turned back north, so we go back and go over the small rise behind the ice house where we can watch for anyone coming in from the north.

As soon as Rhyse spots me up on the ridge, he raises his rifle to shoot. Noah had been tracking him with the scope on his rifle and as soon as Rhyse started raising his, he was dead. Jake was starting to raise his also, and was the next one down. The quiet one threw his rifle down and put his hands up. We walked over to talk to him. We took the weapons and parkas off the bodies and then the shirts, boots and pants. Someone may need them farther down the road.

The other fellow said his name was Joel and he was not part of this bunch at all. He was coming in from out near Manley and they asked him to help them hunt for the girl. He understood she was just lost, not that they were planning on giving her to that low life. We draped the clothes over the garden fence, inside the electric fence and he came in the house with us.

I wanted to know if his story and her story were similar. When he came in with us, she was shy but not afraid, so that was a good sign he was telling the truth. We asked her about him and she said she didn't know who he was. We told her Jake and Rhyse were not going to be a problem any more. Joel offered to take her back home to her Mom and younger siblings, if she wanted to go.

She thought it over a bit and decided yes, she should go home and help her Mom. With those two leeches gone, they could manage and her Mom would need the help. We fixed up some eggs, cheese and milk and loaded it on the sled Rhyse drove over, and she and Joel went back to her home. He looked genuinely upset at the bruises and black eye. That certainly livened up the early winter. I could do without that much excitement.

We haven't heard the pack of wolves howling since we caught 5 in snares a while back. I certainly hope we got the whole pack and not going to have to worry about our animals and even ourselves. So it is a surprise a few days later to see some wolves running through our yard toward the men we left laying in the snow on the hill behind the ice house. One got too close to the electric fence and it nipped him. He yipped and dodged away, so maybe they will stay away, now. After they pass, we set snares along the trail they have used through the edge of our yard.

Evidently, this is a different pack as we have several in snares the next morning, when we get up. The dogs had been very quiet and in their houses, even when we got up, so they had been badly scared during the night. We clear the snares and move them around in different areas, just in case we manage to catch some more. Then we take these in to thaw and skin.

The fur is getting even thicker and close to prime. These are some really good furs so I may use them for the body of Noah's parka I plan on making this winter. The other hides are being tanned now, and we work on them almost every night.

For them to come right through our yard, game must be scarce in the areas around us. We will have to really watch the animals we rely on for our food. I have never seen or heard wolves as many as we have caught, this year.

With not many hunters or trappers the last

few years, their population must have exploded. If they have killed off most of their food supply, they can be very dangerous as they face starvation. We will have to be paying better attention to them.

When Roman and Rose come visiting a couple of days later, they are surprised at how many wolf pelts we already have drying and tanning. We talk over our concerns about how many we are catching and I am not even a very good trapper.

Rose agrees that there seems to be a lot more of them around and we all need to be careful. The people that have cattle and horses need to pay attention and maybe set some snares on trails around their fence lines. With so many people depending on them for food now, we can't afford to lose livestock to wolves, bears or thieves. I don't understand the thieves. Cattle have been given to everyone wanting to raise some, are these people just so used to not working for what they need, that they would rather take the chance on being killed than just do some work? Do they think that if we catch them, we are just going to let them go to come steal from us again?

Chapter 12

We catch 2 more wolves in snares near the house before Thanksgiving. At this rate, we will be making parkas and accessories only out of wolf furs this winter.

We move the snares again and clean up the area where the others were caught. I bring the snares that have caught any into the barn and boil them on the stove in a pan of water and spruce tips. I don't want any wolf scent on the snares when we set them.

Ether we have a lot more wolves moving in than we thought or I am doing a lot better at trapping than I thought I could. We catch 5 more between Thanksgiving and Christmas. This is getting almost ridiculous and they have caught 4 more near the cattle. Everyone is having to be careful leaving their dogs tied outside. It's hard to build fence in the winter with the ground froze solid, but everyone is trying to make it safer for all their animals.

The wolves get into the cattle herd at Liz's and kill 2 before they are shot. Then the cattle have to be butchered out. Not what they wanted to do, late on a full moon night in below zero weather.

We haven't lost any animals but we are keeping most locked in the barn or well fenced yard. The electric fence does help a lot. Once the batteries wear out, we will have to find another means of deterring predators.

We continue to tan the furs we have gotten so far and now are also making a couple of parkas out of the wolf hides. There are a lot of scraps, so they are being used to make mitts and Trapper hats. Noah and I will each have a parka and a small one for Elaine from scraps. I also make Shari's twins each a small parka and an adult sized one for Roman. He is always so helpful and besides, it is always a good thing to keep in good with a father-in-law. Such a nice one is a bonus.

I am making mitts from the face pieces, for all the guys out here that need mitts. After they are done, I braid some moose hide harnesses for them, so they can just slip the mitts off if they need to use their hands for something and have the mitts hanging right there to slip back into. No lost mitts or full of snow from putting them down or dropping them.

I am going to have to start stripping sinew from animals when we butcher to keep a supply of sewing thread on hand for fur sewing. I still have a lot of dental floss, but someday it will run out. From now on, I have to think of everything I use as being limited and it will run out someday. Except maybe that nasty canned tuna I got on sale just before the earthquake. I've seen better looking cat food.

We have mitts and Roman's parka ready by Christmas and we deliver the mitts down at Liz and Richard's place.

I made a small parka for Dan and Melanie's daughter, Patricia. We stop to drop it off and she immediately set up a howl that she didn't like hers, she wanted Elaine's. Time for us to go. Smacking her wouldn't be right, but would sure make me smile.

On our way, we stop at Jeremy and Ashley's place. A very large young man comes to the door behind Jeremy. Elaine is happy to see him, as far as I know, I have never seen him before. Elaine is chattering about her Big Man. They call him Joey.

One look at his child-like face and I know there is nothing to fear from this child trapped in an adult body. Jeremy is almost blushing. It seems the person that was watching us, was this young man. He tried to trade for anything he took and he had not known it was wrong to let Elaine out of her pen while I was working. Jeremy says he seems to be about the level of a happy 6 year old, old enough to understand a lot, but not enough to be more than a large child. Evidently, the couple I shot were the ones keeping him, and had told him to watch our place. He did know they were not his mother and father. He said they made his Mommy and Daddy fall down and not get up again, so he had to go with them. I felt a little bit better about shooting Mrs. Santa after hearing that.

When Jeremy caught him, he wasn't positive about him so never said anything except to tell me my problem was solved. After having him around, he and Ashley both decided they would keep him. For his part, he adored them, followed them around and really was a lot of help. He got right in and did whatever they asked, he was large and strong enough to do a lot.

We continued dropping off packages at the places along our route home. It is always nice to see people we have come to know and like. It is similar to having a large family and we all depend on each other to make it work. We could and would survive out here without everyone else, but it makes our lives so much richer and better to have the community. I was very happy on my own before meeting and getting to know any of these people, yet would miss them all very much, if suddenly left alone again. I can't even imagine life without Noah and Elaine.

When we get home, we do up the evening chores. On the 6th of December, sunrise is at 11:25 am and sunset is at 2:47 pm, so days are getting easier to say I worked from sunup to sundown. By going visiting, we actually worked in the dark, morning and evening. A good thing it is fairly light a couple of hours on each side of actual sunrise and sunset.

When we go delivering packages the other direction, to Al and Natalie, we spend most of the afternoon visiting with them. I finally ask Natalie how she and Amy came to be at the Yukon River, fishing.

"I worked at the café at the bridge, and Amy was a tourist driving north a couple of days before the quake."

"When the quake hit and we listened to the radio a little bit, the rest of the crew headed down to see if there were any boats pulled up along the river. They found a couple and decided the best chance to make it was to float downriver and see if they could move into one of the villages if any survived."

"I didn't have a boyfriend and the other women there, did. So they loaded up the boats with all the food they could carry out of the café and took off, just leaving me at the café."

"They took most of the meat and fresh goods with them, but I still had some left that I stored behind the cabin until it was cold enough to keep in a cool chest on the porch."

"I fixed up one of the rooms and salvaged what I could from the supplies they left behind. Then I thought better of it and moved across the road into the little log cabin the BLM had for tourist information. It had a wood stove in it."

"I stacked all the perishable foods around the walls and dragged a bed over there. I carried as many clothes and blankets as I could and had myself a little nest set up. Then I started cutting and dragging firewood to the cabin and stacking it all around the outside."

"Just before the snow got too deep, Amy came staggering in. She said she was ill and stayed in the cabin while I got more firewood for the winter. Her car ran out of gas somewhere up the road and she had walked for the last several days, she said. Later, I found it just out of sight in the trees to the north of the cabin. It looked like she stayed in it and ran the motor just often enough to keep from freezing until it ran out of gas."

"She watched me set up the cabin to live in then waited until she got too cold to stay there. I found a small boat with oars, and a net in it, so did catch some late salmon to freeze and use during the winter."

"I don't think I would have survived the whole winter except she didn't want to have to do all the work by herself. She usually managed to get hurt or ill any time the work was very hard.."

"We had been arguing when Al, Thad and James showed up to fish. I wanted to catch enough to make the whole winter and she wanted to just catch some, dry them and walk south. She looked at the men as her way out of there and a better life."

"I didn't mind the idea of walking south, but I wanted to have enough food stashed that if we went so far and found no one, we could go back and survive. There should still be a bale of dried salmon in that little cabin. I closed it up good and tight before we left so animals couldn't get in and trash what I left stored in it."

"A person could live in that cabin if they had to. It has a nice heater. It's very small, but easy to heat, too. I even closed the shutters over the windows before I left."

Noah and I look at each other. We had not even checked that little cabin when we made our trip up to salvage goods. It is probably a good idea to leave a cabin well stocked just in case it is ever needed in the future.

It sounded like Amy had been more of a liability to Natalie over the winter than a help. No wonder she was not upset by Amy's demise. Natalie did the work, Amy reaped the benefits. Al had evidently never asked her about it all, so he listened to her story also. Then he asked her why she let Amy stay with them when they first got here. She told him she always tried to think the best of folks and tried not to let her feelings override her wanting everything to be alright. She thought maybe Amy just couldn't handle the remote area and was afraid of being alone.

Maybe she was, but she didn't have an endearing way of showing it.

Chapter 13

Liz, Richard, family and friends make the rounds caroling and it is so unexpected yet lovely and perfect, it brings tears to my eyes. The weather cooperates and it is a fairly warm evening for this time of year. The aurora comes out in full splendor, dancing to the carols. This is one of those moments you want to freeze in your memory to look back on many times throughout the year.

When everyone comes in and warms up a bit on the warm heater benches, we have some mint tea and rehash the year just past and all it has meant to us.

I have some cookies I made as an experiment and we agree they are best dipped in the tea to soften them a bit. The flavor is good, anyway. Some recipes are best forgotten.

I show Liz the calf she brought over almost 2 months ago. The calf is still small for her age, but she is healthy and feisty and still thinks she and the kid goat are sisters. So does the goat.

They are both bucket fed now, and I still

keep them covered with a blanket wrap. Liz says by her markings, she may have some milk producing cows in her ancestry. If so, I may have actual cream to make real butter with in a couple of years. I like the goat butter, but it takes 5 gallons of milk to make 1 pound of the butter. At least I can make some cheese out of the buttermilk.

After Christmas, Annie comes back, with Joel and her mother, Hannah. I am not sure whether she will be upset that we made her a widow, or not, so I don't say anything. She, however, has no doubts about what to say and thanks us very much for that job.

She lets us know they were not married, he just moved himself in and took over. She and her children were his personal slaves. She is overjoyed to be rid of him. She figures anyone else thinking the same way, should be wearing their balls as neckties and she would be willing to help them achieve that end. I tell her she might want to talk to Rose about some special herbs to keep on hand for such a situation in the future. She is of the opinion no one is getting that close again. Joel has taught her how to shoot. She thanks us for saving her daughter and ridding her of the mess she was in. We send them home with more eggs, milk and cheese. They will be building a small barn and planting grain this spring as soon as possible, to get some chickens and maybe a goat of their own, and a cow.

Noah and Joel talked a bit before they left and Joel told him that he and Annie were planning on getting married the following summer.

We catch a couple more wolves and so does Liz and Richard around the cattle. They don't lose any more cattle, though. I boil up the carcasses and feed the chickens. They don't mind the flavor. The ravens and jays feed on the rest.

Our days settle into a routine that we enjoy. We wake up to Elaine chatting to herself in her room. Noah fixes the fire and I get her out of bed and we go to the living room. She loves the warm benches to get dressed on.

I start breakfast while Noah brings in the eggs and feeds and waters the chickens and turkeys. We have them separated in the coop by putting chicken wire down the middle of the coop. We can still feed, water and gather eggs from the sun porch without going into the coop. While he is on the sun porch, he checks the plants and waters any needing it. The LED lights are turned on for the birds.

After breakfast, one of us does the milking and feeds the calf and kid goat. The other dresses Elaine and takes her with them to feed the dogs and clean the runs. It's far easier to keep them clean all winter than to be cleaning it as it thaws in the spring and is nauseating. No smell when frozen. We have an area where we dump the buckets as we fill them and add ashes from the heater over them. It helps.

If there is fresh snow, we all shovel the yard and to the barn.

When we go in, we warm up a bit on the benches and then we start our daily reading lesson. Yes, I know she is too young to read, but she enjoys it and I enjoy reading to her. I use my finger to follow along as I read and she watches it closely.

Then we have some soup for lunch and she goes down for a short nap. Noah and I have been working a lot on the hides we are tanning and making clothing from. Our leather from the moose hide we got from Al is not all that soft, but we make some pants out of it, anyway. They should last almost forever. Once it softens up enough from wearing them, they should get more comfortable. We use the rolls of fake sinew I had from crafting work I used to do. It is like industrial dental floss. I hope it wears as well.

A couple of the wolf hides were not good fur, so we made leather out of them, also. I make a small outfit for Elaine out of it. She wouldn't be able to move in the moose hide. I use the thickest areas of the moose hide for the front of the legs.

By the time Elaine wakes up, my fingers are sore from pushing a needle through and so are Noah's. We are getting calluses. We have some moccasins cut out to sew from the moose hide, also.

She was easier to housebreak than the puppies. Of course, with her parents always near and paying attention, it is easier than when everyone held down jobs outside the home, no one was paying that much attention to the baby and it was easier to just slap another diaper on. Having to hand wash diapers speeds up the training process, also.

We gear up again to bring in firewood for the next day and what we will use tonight. Then go out to feed and clean the barn, milk and feed the calf and kid. By the time we get back in the house, it is fairly late. Time to start dinner. Usually that is simple as we keep a pot of something or other cooking on the heater all the time. But we set the table and bring bread, butter, and whatever is on the stove over to the table.

We talk to each other over dinner, including Elaine in our conversation. She loves this time of day. Soon, we are finished and we clear the table and do the day's dishes. We usually play some game or read a bit more, then sing while we get Elaine ready for bed. She still loves to hear her Daddy sing her to sleep.

After she is settled in bed, we either play a game of cards or read to ourselves. If we have some skinning or tanning going, we work on that. Some days, especially if we have shoveled snow, we don't make it past Elaine's bedtime. One of us stokes up the fire and the other builds one last fire in the mass heater. Then it is off to bed for the night.

It is a satisfying routine and we enjoy it. Noah's ribs have healed up nicely, no pain left at all. So we are healthy and having a good winter.

Shari is pregnant again and not having as bad a time as she did, last time. She says it better be only one, this time. She says sure she is, now the twins are both potty trained and talking well, starting to help around the house and she could enjoy them and now she is going to have another one.

Everyone starts gathering up the baby clothes to take back to her. They have been washed and mended when needed. I make a few more blankets, baby sized from the stuff we cleaned up after bringing it home from the Yukon. Most has good sections to them, just right for children's or babies blankets. They are all the same color, but it isn't like we have a lot of choice. I do make some dye out of onion skins to make pale yellow sheets. Not much of a change, but still a change.

The rodents had chewed some of the quilts and sheets quite badly, and the material that was left I cut into pieces as large as I could, trimming away the chewed areas. These pieces, I used to make clothing for the children. I was also making boxers for Noah. I didn't have elastic, so they are just drawstring. He says it is better than none. I've made a couple of pairs for myself. They are not much better than none. My attempts to make myself a bra are not all that funny. But we laugh at them, anyway. After I check in a mirror, yeah, they are that funny.

We keep finding projects to keep us busy all winter. We have several that we want to get done this summer, also. We will try to start some before the growing season hits and we are swamped trying to make sure we have enough growing to keep us healthy and to supply seed for the season after.

Rose found a canister of black oil sunflower seeds she had for feeding the birds. The seed is a few years old, and not sure how much of it will sprout, but we each take some to try. If we can get it to produce, we can make sunflower oil from the seeds. They are so high in oil content, that it practically oozes out if they are warmed. I presprout a few on paper towels and get about 50% sprout rate. Good enough. I start them in little containers of soil on the sun porch. 2 weeks later, I start a few more. Some I will plant in the greenhouse and some outdoors near the house and barn.

I went through all my trash, right after the earthquake and took out all the cans and bottles. Most of the cans, I cut the tops off and now use to start plants in, with a hole punched in the bottom. The plastic bottles are used the same. The larger clear ones have the bottoms cut out and I use them as mini-greenhouses over plants planted outdoors, early. I remove the lids during warm days and replace at night. They will eventually fall apart from being out in the sun, but I store them in the dark of the old ice house after they have been used in the spring.

The sun porch is getting to be hazardous to walk through, with all the little seedlings in various stages of growth.

We start tapping the birch trees just as early as possible. Spring is warming up fairly fast, but still freezing at night, so we are getting a lot of sap. The little sugar shack is busy as we try to keep it boiling night and day without burning any.

We have an area cleared out of snow and have packed buckets of gravel over to make a building pad so we can start making a mass heater greenhouse. Roman brings over several windows we can use to help us along. I have several left down in my building salvage piles. We are going to try making clay pipes for the chimney needed in the benches since we don't have that much metal pipe laying around for what we want to do. If it develops a crack in the greenhouse, it won't kill us in our sleep like it could in the house. We make it in sections so they will slide together. We make the firebox out of homemade clay bricks, also. We bake them a while in our heater to make them hard at least, before using in our construction. We do this with the pipe sections, also. No use squashing them as we are constructing this.

We leave the caps off the ends of the cleanouts we build in, so we can keep checking to make sure we don't squash our pipes or bricks. We put the caps in place and start fires now and then to keep drying and toughening up the inside of our work in progress. We cover it at night in an attempt to keep it from freezing and developing a spongy texture to the COB. We won't get an early start planting in it this season, but maybe we can add time to the end of the season, using it.

We are mixing the COB in the tub, but have it inside the greenhouse next to our building site. If I have to dance around in my holey shorts in muck, I would like to be out of sight of anyone coming in our driveway unexpectedly. I keep a piece of cloth handy

to wrap around like a sarong just in case.   I
am trying to keep me as entertainment down
to a minimum.

We are going to open the side of this
greenhouse to the new one, when we get it
mostly built, so it gets heated better, also.

Of course, someone does show up, so I am
busy trying to get the muck washed off my
legs and wrapped in the cloth before they get
completely to the yard. There wasn't time to
heat the water I was using, so it is icy cold and
not doing much for my frame of mind.
When I come out and find Melanie and her
spoiled little daughter there, I am tempted to
just keep working in the mud.

She surprises me by starting to cry and
asking for help to teach her daughter better
behavior. This would be a chore, since the
child has been given anything she desires and
then some. That is pretty hard to do out here
in these circumstances, but Melanie has
managed it. She refused to allow Dan to
correct the child at any time. I am hesitant to
tell her how I would go about it.

So, since Elaine is napping and we have a
little time before she will wake up, we go in
and I fix some tea. As I am putting some
cookies out, Patricia slaps my hand away and
grabs for the plate. I slap her hand right back,
tell her NO and put the plate out of reach.
She immediately starts to tear up and open

her mouth to scream and I tell her No in a firm voice. She stops and looks at me and starts to open wide again.. I say No, again, in a firm voice and tell her if she wants tea and cookies with the rest of the grownups, she has to use good manners. She stops and thinks this over. She is a very intelligent little girl, just badly spoiled, but she understands when talked to.

She sits by her mom and drinks her tea that is about half milk and eats her cookie. I make her say please and thank you and she does it nicely. Melanie is surprised and wants to know if I would keep her child a while. I tell her they always behave better for someone else than for a parent and she would just go back to being her usual self even if she did behave here for me.

I tell her she will just have to be consistent most of all and not give in just because the child is screaming and wearing her out. Make there be consequences to her actions and do it every single time, no exceptions. She says she will have a hard time but that Dan is all for it. He is getting irritated at how badly his daughter behaves and she hasn't let him do anything to correct her.

She says she grew up in a regimented household where children were seen but not heard. Every little thing was cause for punishment and never forgotten to be brought up over and over. She just couldn't do that to her child.

Well, I agree, no child should have that kind of treatment either, but there is a happy medium. Listening to her talk about her childhood made me understand Melanie a lot better.

Elaine woke up just as they were getting ready to leave. I waited until they were out the door before going in to get her up. I just didn't want to deal with it today.

Noah and Dan had stayed outside and worked on the greenhouse while we were in the house visiting. Evidently Dan told Noah why they were here and hoped I could get through to Melanie how to fix the problem a bit. He loved them, but he couldn't take having such a spoiled little girl and a nervous wreck of a wife much longer. Trapping on the Porcupine River seemed a lot more attractive at the moment.

We went back to mixing COB and Elaine got right in, slapping it on the benches. We started a fire in it and put a pan of water to heat on top for the next cleanup. We had the benches almost finished now and would begin building the greenhouse frame over them. Dan and Noah had put together some of the sections and all we would have to do is stand them up in place and nail them down. The end with the firebox would be against an outer wall of the chicken coop, so maybe we could warm it some in winter while growing food.

We managed to finish our last batch of COB muck on the firebox and benches, clean ourselves off and get in the house without any more interruptions.

The next day, we built planter boxes on top of the benches. We would line them with plastic and make a drain out the lower ends with some of the old hose we had on hand. We caulked around it, so leakage wouldn't affect the COB under it. Then we started filling the planter beds. Some gravel in the very bottom on top of some straw to keep it from puncturing the plastic. Then the cleanings from the chicken coop and barn from last year. Then soil on top, several inches deep with some ashes mixed in to sweeten it up some and stop moss growth.

Then the wall sections went up and we covered them with plastic. After the plastic, we put some fiberglass panels we had, on the roof over the plastic so it is double layer with air between. The glass windows went in the south facing walls. We would cut the plastic out over the windows on the inside and make frames to place it back when the weather turned cold in the fall. We brought out some of the plants we had started on the sun porch and planted them in the new beds. This would house our winter squash as we only had a few seeds left and the ones we got from Liz. If these didn't make viable seeds, we may never have more winter squash. At each corner, I planted 2 of the sunflower plants with cucumbers planted around the sunflowers.

So much depended on each crop not only producing, but producing enough viable seed for us to save for the next seasons crops with enough to share an keep extra in case we couldn't get a crop next year.

We couldn't dwell on it, all we could do was our best not to let anything happen to our crops and supplies.

Chapter 14

Two nights later, we get a late snowstorm and spend most of the night, stoking fires in the greenhouses. By morning, it is 20 degrees F. and everything has almost 2 foot of snow on it. We keep stoking the fires all day and shoveling snow off the roofs as this is a late wet snow and heavy. The trees are starting to green up nicely and this breaks a lot of limbs heavy with sap and new leaves.

Down at Liz and Richards, their main problem are the new calves. They spend most of the night and next day making sure the calves are all safe and in the shelters around the barns. They still have some hay left, so are feeding it out. A pack of wolves comes over the berm near their house, headed for the barns and cattle when Liz and Richard both open fire. They manage to kill several and the few remaining get on the other side of the barn and running down the valley where Mike and his sister takes up and gets the rest of the pack. One cow was injured as a wolf slashed her leg a bit as it ran by, which is how wolves usually slow down their prey enough to catch up and feed on them. They doctored the cow and she would be okay.

Within a week, the snow is gone, again, and we get back to planting. We drag the areas we want to plant to grain and scatter the composted dog and cat refuse mixed with ashes over and drag the areas yet again with the dogs pulling the drag. We wait a few days, then scatter the seed and drag it again to get the seed out of sight of the birds coming through in flocks, migrating farther north. We have made a roller out of an old barrel, to drag behind the dogs, also, and it is filled with water to add some weight and press the seeds in better. The dogs are getting a workout today and loving it.

The plants and seeds in the greenhouses are popping up out of the ground. The heated beds are amazing. I think I can actually watch the squash plants grow as their tendrils reach out. The cucumbers are doing the same. We may be making pickles this year. The dill patch has reseeded itself and is coming up very well in the herb garden. The leaf lettuce stuck in along the sides is ready to thin, so we will have very small salads with our evening meal.

It's not even June yet and we have next year's firewood in, the gardens and greenhouses planted and we are feeling proud of ourselves.

Before the ice goes out on the creeks we decide to drive up to the Yukon River and see what is left at the old Pump Station and the camp. Roman wants to go with us, so we decide to go the next day.

We go across the ice on the river first, and check around the old buildings to see if there is anything we can use at home, short of dismantling the buildings and taking them. The guys actually consider this, but maybe next year. We check the little cabin Natalie and Amy spent the winter in, and leave it stocked and closed up, just in case someone needs it.

We find more blankets and quilts in the stock room of the old motel. We have Roman's trailer on the other side of the river and haul mattresses, and bedding across the ice and start loading it.

One of the small metal buildings is about to collapse, so the men disassemble it and we load it, also. Under it, they find some tools and several old sets of springs from trucks. Those go on our load, also. Roman wants the tire shop tools and compressor, so it is loaded. We even load one of the generators.

By the time we finish looking through the camp, we have a lot of items loaded. We then go up to the Pump Station. None of our people have really searched through it. Noah and I found the loader right out by the gate and took it home. We did not go inside the gates. The snowplow was outside the gate, also.

We are amazed at what has been left here. We stock up on dry goods from the kitchen store rooms. All sorts of kitchen utensils, pots and pans are here. We sort through and take a good supply. The medic's office has a locked cabinet of medicines and we take the whole cabinet off the wall. We pack up all the supplies in the office, including the tools and exam table. Out behind the buildings, we find another tractor trailer loaded with dry food supplies. Oh yeah, that is going home with us, if we can get it started.

Roman is a whiz on diesel mechanics and Noah is no slouch, himself. Soon they have it running and we decide our trip has been a success.

Roman airs up all the tires that are low on the tractor trailer and he will drive it home. We will follow along behind, pulling our loaded trailer. While going around a long sloping curve, I notice a vehicle off the side of the road on the far side. We stop when we get there and go investigate. There are a few bones scattered around, but nothing fresh. There is a rifle in the front seat and a handgun on the console between the seats. Behind the seat is several boxes of ammunition for both. There is also a very good parka, mitts and winter boots behind the seat. The backpack in the passenger seat is loaded with clothing and dry food for a week. A typical vehicle for anyone living in the Bush.

This has been here quite a while and was only visible from that one spot when I happened to be looking. We add all of this to our load and the spare tire from in back, it will fit my pickup. A little farther down the road and we are glad we did, we have a blowout. The end of a culvert is poking through the road and we hit it.

By the time we catch up with Roman, he was about to come back looking for us. We show him our new supplies.

By the time we get home, Elaine has been asleep in her seat for most of the return trip and is wide awake. We, however, are so ready for bed. But we have chores to do yet and a meal to prepare. Roman parks the tractor trailer unit along the road out front and Noah takes him home while I milk. Elaine goes with them so I can rush through the outside chores.

By the time I get back inside, Noah and Elaine are home and I pull the pot of stew off the heater to reheat for dinner. It is still warm, so doesn't take long.

After we eat, we all go to bed. This has been a long arduous day on all of us. Of course we have someone at the door bright and early the next morning. Al has come by to see what we found and wants to check out the load in the trailer on the tractor out by the roadway. He heard it come by last night and could hardly wait to come see what we found.

We all get dressed and Roman and Rose show up. So it is time to go see exactly what all we have found this time. We only opened the doors, saw it was fully loaded and brought it home.

When we open the doors this time, we are pleased to see that it seems to all be dry goods so nothing would have frozen and broke to ruin anything. Even the cooking oils are in fine shape. There are enough spices to stock everyone up for several years. Sugar and flour, yeast, baking powder, baking soda, rice and noodles. It is all packed in so tightly, we can't really tell the extent of our haul. We close the doors and go unload the trailer behind the pickup.

After it is unloaded, we start unloading some of the items from the big trailer. We start a pile for each household and add to it depending on the size of the household. As we dig deeper into the load, we find 25 pound boxes of chocolate chips. We will set those aside to break them up into smaller containers to share with everyone. 50 pound bags of brown sugar, cooking cocoa and of powdered sugar are a surprise, also. This must have been the stocking up order for baking for the winter for all the Pump Stations.

The items that were plentiful, we just left in their original bags and boxes to take to the other households. We are making a list of the other items we will have to share and asking each household to supply containers to put theirs in.

There are even cans of powdered eggs for baking. Since we now have chickens, those aren't as precious as they would have been, without the chickens, but we will still share and keep a supply for ourselves. Until opened, they last almost forever.

The medical supplies we haul down to Richard. We can all chip in time and help build a small cabin to have as a clinic. Since we brought the exam table also and a chair we found in the office, he is set. The reflector and assorted other supplies are all in the pickup. He is surprised at how much we managed to bring back with us. Noah told him we did leave the walls.

We leave a supply of the bedding from the old motel, along with a few of the beds. With all the folks they have there, they need more beds and bedding. If we build a clinic, he may want at least a couple of beds in it.

By the time we sort through almost everything in the large trailer, it is getting tedious. But we find more surprises in the boxes of flaked coconut and lemon crystals. There are 5 gallon tins of coffee, tea and hot chocolate mixes. Powdered fruit and breakfast drinks are well represented, also. This is beyond our wildest dreams on food supplies at this point. We start delivering the basic piles of supplies so they don't get wet if it rains or heavy dew falls during the dusk that is night now. There is several hundred pounds of flour and sugar, so every household gets quite a bit. We let them know they will have to supply containers for the other stuff and go on to the next place. Al takes his supply home and says he will be back the next day to help. Roman and Thad take theirs and also for Rose and for Kara and all the ones she feeds. Kara and Liz get the most of any item as they feed the most people.

I'm thinking the trailer would be very nice as an addition to our outbuildings around here. It is weatherproof and metal so fairly fire proof too. We can dig trenches to park the tires in, and have it closer to the ground without setting it directly on the ground and allowing rodents to find entry into it, somehow.

Maybe we should remove the tires and block it on the axles. The tires might fit the backhoe or some of the tractors Liz and

Richard brought up. No use letting them rot into the ground.

Roman is building another shop. This one will hold the tire tools and assorted other equipment he picked up at the river camp and pump station. He is building his own little industrial village there at the top of Rose's driveway. It is set out very orderly and neat. He has his welding shop, his mechanics shop, his building supply shop and wood working shop. The man knows how to do almost everything. His sons are right there along with him on being handy and knowing how to work.

The day "Government Guy" decided to come out here and then bring his family along was one of those days that just usually happen to other people.

Chapter 15

I'm thinking that with all these new supplies, we should build a cache of some sort with enough supplies in it to see our community through some hard times if needed. Maybe that is what this trailer should be used for, instead of keeping it in our yard. It would withstand some fire, rodents and is weatherproof. That is better than almost anything we could build. I talk to Noah about it and he agrees, we should do something like that.

We haven't handed out all the staples yet, so we will just keep quite a bit back and also on the shares of the items we haven't divided yet. We will just put entire boxes of some of the goods back and not add them into the shares to give out. Not even for ourselves.

When Al shows up the next day to help us sort and distribute, we tell him our plan. He agrees we should do that. After all, we could have just kept this all to ourselves but we are sharing and making sure everyone gets some of each item.

He suggests we bury the container into the

side of a hill, so it stays cooler in summer and not so apt for anything to go rancid, since it is all already a few years old.

I don't really have any place suitable for that, so we go ask Rose if it can be stashed in the hillside below her house. She agrees and says she will pick off anyone tampering with it from her upstairs window. It is hard to believe she is in her 70's.

We start up the tractor and Roman drives it over to Rose's place. We have all the supplies out that we want to divide up, so they padlock the doors and Roman digs back into the hill better, with the backhoe. Then backs the trailer fairly close, they unhook the trailer and Roman uses the backhoe to turn the trailer and push it into place, with the back end out so it can be opened in the future. Then they cover the trailer with roofing membrane after removing the tires and wheels and blocking it up. Covering it up doesn't take very long.

Now we have a nice tractor with a large sleeper unit on it. There is a microwave and a fridge even, in the sleeper. Several books and clothing. This was someone's home away from home. There are bags of candy and energy bars in the console. Most of the candy is okay, the energy bars are a bit stale.

I find a small handgun stashed in the seat cover on the drivers side. That is a surprise as the truckers were not supposed to be armed.

I am surprised he left it when they all went downriver. There is even ammunition in the pocket on the door, not in a box, just loose so it wasn't noticeable. There is also a very sharp wicked looking knife in the same door pocket. These things come in the house with me. I place the gun, ammo and knife in a small locking tote and put them out in the ice house. I like having things handy no matter where I might be when they are needed.

The handgun from the pickup we found gets stashed in a grain barrel in a bag, out in the feed room in the barn. The rifle is wrapped and put in the rafters of the barn. We wear handguns while working outdoors, mostly because of bears. But it is comforting to know we have more handy if we need them.

We continue working on the garden and clean out the barn and chicken coop. We let the barn animals out in the pens during the day and they can feed on the grass growing around the area. They are not happy to have to go back in the barn at night, but it is safest, by far. Spring bears wouldn't mind a captive meal, neither would the wolf packs still roaming around. We hear them howling at night sometimes, so we know there are still too many around.

Once we get going on sorting through the piles of goods still in our house, we find a few items we will prepare only at holidays and share around. There isn't enough to dole out as they are. What I thought were all 5 gallon buckets of cooking oil seems to have other supplies in some of the cartons covering the buckets.

Someone must have had a lucrative smuggling operation going in the camps. There is enough varieties of alcohol to stock a small liquor store. The vodka will come in handy to make cough syrup and tinctures for medicines. The brandy will make excellent mincemeat. Rum can be boiled down with some sugar and butter to make candy with. I suppose we could use it as trade goods sometime in the future, but I am not sure I want folks coming around for alcohol and then becoming a problem because of it. I certainly don't want to be known as a supplier of it.

I guess in a worst case scenario, it could be used to clean wounds. We will just store it in the back of the ice house. Out of sight should be okay and we are glad we have moved it before anyone comes visiting.

The worst item we found was a bag of cocaine. We decided that should be saved to be used as a medical supply if ever needed. No wonder our trucker carried a gun. When we looked farther in the sleeper unit, we found large quantities of cash in the fridge.

We take the cocaine to Richard to keep with the other medical supplies in the locked cabinet. The key had been on a hook right beside the locked cabinet, so we brought it also.

After these finds, we decided maybe we better check in all the containers that were not sealed. Boxes were opened and contents checked, buckets that were not sealed were opened. I'm just hoping we didn't deliver any of these goods to unsuspecting neighbors.

After these discoveries, we search the tractor with an eye to finding all it's secrets. We do find some compartments that most trucks do not have. One contained several handguns, another, ammunition for them. Just who was this guy and what was he setting up? Guess the earthquake messed up his plans big time. The last compartment we open, we go get Jeremy to take care of.

It appears to be packed with explosives. He says if we had not already disconnected the truck batteries, we probably would now be a small crater here by the road. The little box of odd looking things I couldn't figure out are the timers, primers and fuse or whatever they use now. Then he searches the truck even better and finds a small rocket launcher and rockets along the frame and under the front end. I wonder what all we have buried over at Rose's house?

Well, if we ever need it, we certainly are better armed than the usual little Bush community. Jeremy says he would just as soon stash these here if we don't mind. He already has a large supply taken from the ambushers camp a few winters ago and don't want to have all the stuff in one place. He wants to divide up his supplies and have Roman, Will, Mike and Al take some, also. He would rather we all have some available and never need it. He will show us how to use everything.

It seems like summer is rushing past. By the time we get everything done with the tractor trailer unit, the snow is gone entirely and the ice gone out of the rivers. We still get small earthquakes that seem to have no pattern at all. The river below us seems to be getting deeper. The men drag the fish wheel down to the bank and tow it out a ways with the boat. Then wings are constructed to channel the fish into it, since this is a clear water river and fish can see the paddles. Fish wheels work best in murky streams where the fish can't tell they are about to be scooped up.

Since we won't be staying at the wheel all the time, it has a bin under water to keep the fish alive and swimming around in it until someone dips them out and harvests what we need. Maybe it won't draw scavengers and predators alike. While the boat is being used, a couple of the people want to go exploring a bit and see just how the rivers have changed.

When they get farther down the valley, the water opens up and is flat open water all the way around, where it used to be valley. Either the ground has sunk, or the water levels have risen, a lot. The water tastes brackish, so it may have some salt content.

They have a time finding their way back to our little area. Everything has changed so much. They are running low on fuel when they return and they have seen a lot of nesting ducks, geese and other waterfowl along the edges of the large inland lake or whatever this is, now. They have not seen any sign of other people.

Someone checks the box on the fish wheel every day until we start getting fish, then it is back to someone being handy all the time to take care of the fish as caught. We prepare the salmon strips from the Kings, and start smoking them as soon as they are caught and prepared. We fillet them, cut into strips, soak in a brine solution of salt and brown sugar, then allow to drip dry before smoking until done. If they are to be canned, they are only half dried before processing.

The rest of the fish, we clean, fillet but leave the tail attached and cut the flesh on the side down to the skin in slashes across the fillets. Then hang by the tail over poles in the smoke house. We have constructed some little trapper type cabins for the crews to stay in near the landing. It makes it easier to rest between boatloads out of the bugs and maybe even nap a little bit.

The next time I see Shari, she tells me they heard on the shortwave radio that there has been a lot of disease out in the rest of the world. What the quakes and rioting didn't kill off, the diseases have. People bunching together, without good hygiene sets them up for that. Rats have infested areas with larger populations, spreading disease and ruining food supplies. In some areas, people are living like feral beasts, running in packs and demolishing anything they come across. Cannibalism has been suspected.

It seems that by living in a remote area and not having a large population near or around us may be the best thing we could have done to enjoy a long life. Well, other than the occasional pesky low life that drops by or tries to overrun us. I'm still having a time coming to terms with Mrs. Santa, she looked so sweet and nice. The gun she pulled on me said otherwise. That is a sure way to feed the ravens.

Joel, Annie and Hannah come over early in the summer to see about driving some cattle over towards Manley. Joel says there are several families still over there and they could use the cattle and a few chickens if we had any to spare. Richard had never made it on out to Manley in all the times he came up to visit, so he and Liz decided they could join a drive on out. They can take crates with chickens and a few turkeys on one of the wagons with a team. Several of the others would like the chance to try trail herding cattle, even if it is only a few and want to go, also.

We load them up with supplies and they trail out about the time the fish wheel was put in the river but before the fish started running.

The cattle are feisty and they push them almost 20 miles the first day, then they settle down and make 10 to 14 per day the rest of the trip. They find the first family settled on the Hutlinana and spend a night there. They would like a couple of cows but don't have enough area to cut hay yet. They will, next season, if they can come get one or two, then. They do ask for a couple of the hens and a rooster. They are already building a small coop as they talk.

The next couple of families are at Baker Creek. They have redone the old gardens and greenhouse the old man used to have there, years ago. They do have enough area to cut hay and are thrilled to get a couple of cows and some chickens.

When they get farther down the road, they meet some folks heading out the road toward Baker Creek. As soon as they find out what the deal is on the cows, they turn right around and accompany them back toward Manley. The river is a lot higher than it used to be there, also and now the hot springs are almost at the edge of the river. There are still a few families living in the area and they are willing to start cutting hay as soon as it is ready. Liz and Richard give them a quick course in caring for the animals and how to feed in the winter and building shelters for them.

They leave 10 cows and a bull for them to share. The chickens and turkeys are to be community property until there are enough for each family to have a few. Some of the hens are broody, and Liz brought a basket of fertile eggs along, so they are put to set as soon as they are in the shed to be used as a coop for now.

The upper greenhouses have been repaired after the quakes and are still working and have ripe tomatoes to share, so they load up the wagon with baskets of tomatoes to take home and can. Those will be welcome by everyone. The trip home doesn't take as long and they stop at each place they left cows or chickens to see how they are doing. They are home in 4 days. A few of the tomatoes have bruises, but everyone here is so happy to see them that no one minds. The lettuce heads and other fresh produce sent our way is welcome as none of our gardens have started producing much, yet. We do have leaf lettuce and are using it, but a change is always nice. Fresh salads using fresh tomatoes and lettuce is our menu for a few nights with a few things added. Our sandwiches feature them, also.

Chapter 16

In late July, we start cutting hay. Noah and I have to take turns as Elaine is too heavy now to carry while cutting and it's too dangerous to let her play around where we are cutting. So while one of us cuts, the other has Elaine while doing something else, like weeding, in the garden or greenhouses.

I am hand pollinating and keeping certain squashes covered in a cloth bag until they set, then marking to keep separate and save seeds from them. We need seeds for next year for everyone. The mass heater has done well getting them off to a quick start and all the fertilizer buried under them is doing it's job, now. That greenhouse has become a total jungle of huge squash plants and sunflowers growing at each corner. The cucumbers are also climbing the sunflowers, and I have to keep the squash vines moved away or they would choke them all out.

We have the marked cucumbers maturing to save seeds from, but I am picking and making pickles every other day. I have even had Rose and Liz come pick for pickle making. We are getting bumper crops of everything. The corn is setting ears and looks like a good crop, also. We have marked the earliest ears to allow to mature for seed.

Elaine still gets stuck in the pen with the baby goats, so she enjoys playing with them or the puppies.

While I am pollinating some squash, I hear her scream and it is not a play scream it is a scream of fear.

I am around the open door of the greenhouse with my gun drawn and am face to face with a very large bear. I don't even stop to think, I punch it right in the soft nose with the gun in my hand. Back inside the greenhouse with the door slammed between us and out the other end of the greenhouse and scooping up Elaine. We hit the open door of the barn and I have it slammed shut behind us just as fast and up the ladder to the upper floor. Then I put a howling Elaine on a bale of straw, tell her to stay and open the haymow to see where the bear is and what he is doing. He is looking over our little goats in the pen, so I take careful aim and shoot him.

Elaine and I wait in the loft a while, to make sure he really is dead. Noah heard the shot and comes in the drive at a run. I hold up my hand in the loft and he sees me. I point down where the bear is, so he comes around and up where we are. We sit and wait a while longer, then he goes down and uses a long stick to poke the bear in the eye. If it is alive, that will always get a response. Better then, than while we are skinning it and have it half undressed.

Elaine and I went down the ladder and got the skinning supplies and a tarp. She went back into the goat pen and we skinned the bear and took the meat in the house. We cut it into sections and put it in the ice house to cool.

I mix up some cure to start it curing with and put that on it. We will flesh the hide out better, tonight.

Noah takes over at the house and I go cut hay a while. I need the rest.

By the time we quit for the day, we are both worn out and so is Elaine. So we put the animals back in the barn, feed and water everything and go indoors. The hide is waiting for us to flesh it out. I salt it down and roll it up. It will last a day or two longer that way. We eat a quick dinner and go to bed.

The next morning, I redo the meat in the cure while I am out feeding the animals and letting them out for the day. We will drag the gut pile away somehow, today.

We have the gut pile in a large tub out behind the barn, when Al pulls in with his little goat cart he built. His goats are now trained as a team and pull quite well.

He asks if we have been bothered by a bear recently and we say yes, we have. The gut pile is behind the barn. He describes the bear and it sounds like the same one. He relaxes and says okay, it has been stalking them around their place and they never could get a clear shot at it. He offers to dump the tub over the edge of the road, between our places and bring the tub back later. We accept.

For a guy that didn't like people, he certainly has come out of his shell. From an almost hermit existence to married with a child and another young man he adopted, sort of. I think he is the best neighbor I have ever had and there are some really nice ones around us, now.

When he brings the tub back the next morning, he says nope, it wasn't the same one. They are skinning theirs out, right now and would I cure and smoke it with ours?

Sure, since I will be doing that anyway. More meat won't take much extra than what I am already doing. He says he will be right back.

It is actually a couple of hours later when he brings the pieces of meat back to be cured and smoked. But he has trimmed and cleaned them up so they look very nice. Not a hair on the meat. I have never had such clean meat brought to me to work with. So it is simple to just take it to the ice house and add it to the one I have curing. He likes the way I have the ice house set up and asks how I constructed it. He doesn't have any permafrost areas on his place, so that limits how close to mine he can manage.

After he leaves, Noah and I start leveling out an area to construct another greenhouse. If we are going to have to rely on only ourselves out here, we are going to need to be assured we can produce enough food. We can't be depending on suddenly finding more sources that are still good, cached around along the roads.

The mass heater is doing such a good job, we will incorporate them into all the future greenhouses we build and probably any other cabins. We found a wide vein of clay on the bank of the roadbed across the road from our driveway, so we will be using that for the COB.

Roman has a stack of the clear panels for building greenhouses and he shares with us and Rose. They are building more over at her place, using our heater design. Her sister is building a large greenhouse on their place from the materials they picked up in town on their way out. They are also building in a mass heater. By using clay to make all the pipes, we can make as many as we want with no worry about running out of materials for that.

The fish wheel is catching enough that no one will be out netting this season. That frees up people to work on the gardens and construction of houses, barns and shops. Whenever a house or other building is due to go up, we try to all show up and make it happen in a day or so. We are getting it down to a science.

Liz is teaching others how to train horses, not only to saddle but to harness, also. If we must go back a few centuries in technology, horses will be a very important part of the success of the communities. She and Richard have laid the groundwork for successful communities all along the trail they made coming up.

One of the old books in Rose's library mentions tanning leather using urine, in Europe. I knew the old time Eskimos used it, for their tanning, but was not aware it was common in other countries, also. Not something I really want to try, but I guess that is needed, so we don't use up our salt supplies on leather instead of food. Oh ugh.

Thad and Noah are experimenting on building vats using electrical wire to bind the slats together. Varying sizes would have a lot of uses. Someday, our plastic buckets are all going to wear out. This would be a start of making small ones with handles for buckets.

They immediately start trying to make buckets. I really appreciate the ones they have me try out. Yes, they are heavier than the plastic ones, but they should last almost forever if taken care of. This is excellent and they take some over to share with the other households.

Dan has some rolls of wire he donates to their project. Will has some 1x4 inch hardwood boards he gives them to see about making some household buckets. Al knows where a roll of the old telegraph wire is located, near his winter trapline. He will load it up and bring it in, next winter. It will make sturdy handles and bindings for large vats.

Telegraph lines were being stretched across Alaska to the Bering Sea, then under the sea and across Siberia, until a cable was placed across the Atlantic and stopped the telegraph line. Wire can still be found in areas of Alaska dating from that time. It is a very heavy non insulated wire and handy for a lot of projects. To find a whole roll was a treasure for certain. It's funny what has become treasures to us now.

Jeremy and Dan want to build a mill along the river somewhere. They think they can use it in the summer to grind grain. They are not sure what to use for the stones, but figure if they can manage a system to produce power of some sort, they will figure out a grinding system. Their worst problem will be ice damage in winter and spring.

No one knows just what happened, but the smokehouse by the river, full of fish smoking, drying and dried has burned. This is terrible but no one was hurt. However, if we don't manage to replace the fish, we may have to kill off a lot of our dogs. The dogs are our main transportation all winter, besides being part of the community. No one wants to even consider this. So we try thinking of ways to replace the fish. The fish wheel is placed back in the river and a crew also goes out in the boat with the nets to set across some of the other streams not too far from us.

The catch is disappointing. The Kings are long gone and the Silvers are not lagging far behind them. The crews stay at it 24 hours a day, hoping to recover at least enough for the dogs. They are setting the nets near a new creek mouth when they spot some bundles on the bank. When they pull in, they look just like the bundles we had in the smokehouse and lost in the fire.

They find a path leading toward our set up and surprise the ones rebuilding the smokehouse when they come out of the brush right beside them. They ask the crew to follow them and everyone does, right back to the bundles. One of the women yells

"Hey, that's my poofy knots you all make fun of me for."

Okay, we are going to have to go back to keeping watch on our stuff. They load the bundles, all except a broken one they leave for the thieves, into the boat and the crew walks back to the smokehouse while the boat brings the fish back around. They will be taken home at the end of this shift. With the fish recently caught and the bundles retrieved, there may be enough to feed the dogs for the winter, but it will be close. All that was lost was not recovered, but enough to make a difference in keeping our dogs. But now we know there are still thieves in the area.

Maybe we need to start displaying the thieves we catch, to deter others, like they did in medieval times. I hate to think we are reverting back to that, but what are the alternatives?

Chapter 17

No matter what our good intentions are, on keeping watch better, it is really hard to do in reality. We had good intentions and you know what used to be said about those. The road to hell being paved and all that.

We didn't hear about the first episode, farther down the valley until later. There were injuries, but none of our folks were killed.

I was out in the barn, fairly late, and the goats were acting upset about something. I sat down over near the pen with the kid and calf in it, hoping to settle them down some. The next thing I knew, someone was blundering around in one of the pens and then, "What the H.....OOOF."

Bill E. Goat strikes again. Only one loud, obnoxious, smelly creature allowed in the barn and that is him.

I am up and over the pen wall as fast as I can make it, and land on my knees right in his belly. That knocks what little wind he may have had left, right out of him. Bill is waiting for another chance at him, so I drag him out of the pen and flip on the LED light strip to see just what I have caught.

He seems to be young, but not a kid. Now that I have him caught and still alive, what can I do with him? This has not been a problem in the past. I tie his hands a feet and tether him to the fence. I move a few sections of the electric fence so if he moves around, he will notice right away.

Then I go looking for Noah. I find him behind the barn, stretched out on the ground with a large lump on the back of his head from being hit with some object. Okay, starting to feel less kindly towards our captive. In his favor, Noah is still alive.

Pretty soon I hear muttering and then a yelp from the other side of the barn. The captive is awake and found the fence.

I am having trouble getting Noah awake, though, so he will just have to wait. I go check on Elaine and she is still asleep. When I get back outside, Noah is trying to sit up, but is having trouble getting his balance. This guy must have hit him with more force than just putting him out. Now I worry about concussion and fractured skull.

The guy by the barn is starting to get on my nerves. He is yelling obscenities and I don't want to listen to it. I walk around the corner with my gun in my hand and tell him to shut up or I will help him be a lot quieter. If my husband isn't okay, he is going to wish he was never born.

After looking at my face, he shuts right up. I am not joking and I am not in a good mood. I need to go get help. So I place a noose around my prisoner's neck and tie it to his feet behind him, so he has to stay in a tight position or choke himself. He starts to complain and I yank the knots a bit tighter, he shuts up.

I cover Noah with a quilt and have his feet raised on a pile of straw. He is muttering but not awake and not able to help me get him in the house. I place fencing around him also to protect him from any predators wandering by. I put Pal in with him and tell him to guard.

Then I get Elaine up and we head down the road in my pickup. It would take too long to walk for help. I pull in at Roman's and he comes right over. I ask him to please come help me with Noah. He gets in the pickup and we are on our way back home before I can tell him what has happened.

I drive the pickup as close to Noah as I can, Roman and I manage to lift Noah up into the pickup. The prisoner yells at us to let him loose. Not in this lifetime. I hope the mosquitoes are eating him alive.

We drive straight to Liz and Richard's. They see us pulling in and have heard us coming for quite a ways. No one drives around just for fun any more, so they know something is wrong. By the time we stop at the house, they are all there to see what is wrong.

We bath his head in cold water, hoping to bring the swelling down some. I open a capsule of allergy meds and dump the capsule under his tongue, just in case it helps reduce swelling, also. Some of the guys saddle up and head over to see about the prisoner.

Richard says there really isn't anything he can do, so we load Noah back into the pickup and take him home where at least he will be in familiar surroundings and I can keep an eye on him.

As we drive past the group coming back with the prisoner, he yells, "Amy told us all about you jerks."

What? Whoa, this is yet another result of letting Amy go, alive? Even now that she isn't, she is still causing us problems?

Just who all is "us" and where are they located? I ask Roman and he says he will help me get Noah settled and come back to talk to them and the prisoner. He asks the men if they will wait at his place with the prisoner as he has some questions. They agree and we go on home.

We get Noah settled in the house in bed and I offer to run Roman home, but he says he can use the exercise and will be back later to help me keep an eye on Noah.

I sponge his face and head and dump

another capsule of allergy meds under his tongue. To me, it is supposed to reduce swelling so just in case it might, I will keep dumping the nasty flavored stuff under his tongue to get it into his bloodstream as fast as possible. He reacts to the flavor, so he is still aware on some level or maybe coming out of it a bit.

A couple of hours later, Roman and Thad both come over. Thad goes out to feed and water the animals and check the greenhouses for water.

Roman says Amy told some fine tales of her mistreatment at the hands of the people here, especially me. I did punch her twice in one day, but she earned it.

He finally got the guy thinking when he asked if she did her share of the work, helped herself to the best of everything and took more than her share no matter what? Did she get along with the other folks in camp and did she offer to help, ever? The prisoner was still tied and in one of the sheds by Roman's house.

One of the boys that came over wanted to know how to tie the hangman's noose I fastened the guy up with. It is the only non-slip knot I really know how to tie well, so use it on a lot of things. The prisoner had practically strangled himself with it, trying to get loose before they got here.

The next day, the prisoner told more of his story. When Amy and her crew came raiding, several others stayed in a larger camp, farther away so we wouldn't notice the smoke from their fires. They did hear the explosion of the grenades going off, but by the time they got over where the remains were, the bear had finished the wreckage of the crew. The signs of the plane landing and taking off showed up very well, so they knew we had something to do with everyone being dead.

At first, they were horrified, thinking we had butchered the bodies to use as food.. Then they noticed the bear tracks and someone tracked the direction he went after feeding. Then the bear came back to see who was messing with his cache of food and they shot him.

Roman asked him if Amy shared the large supply of meat and fish she was dropped off with and he said no, she was left, without any food, to starve. So she saved that all for herself, also.

He was upset that their supply of dried fish was gone, now, except the one broken bale and the few bales they managed to get to their camp before the main supply was found and brought back here. Somehow, he felt once they stole something, it was theirs and we had no rights to it. What an entitlement mentality.

That kind of thinking got the world in a lot

of trouble before the earthquake, were we going to have to deal with it even now? People still looking for the easy way to live well without working for it. Do they never learn?

The next couple of days I am in a daze. Noah doesn't show any sign one way or the other of improving. The only good thing I can say is that he also doesn't seem to be getting worse. I think I have found what he was hit with and if so, it is a wonder he is even alive, and must have a very hard head.

Thrown down in Bill E. Goat's pen is my small sledgehammer. It is supposed to be hanging in the shop area in my woodshed. Was I supposed to be next? What about Elaine? No wonder he is still out. Now I want to go use it on the prisoner, so I stay home so I don't give in to temptation.

Roman and Thad come spend time to give me a chance to go outside and take care of the greenhouse and gardens. Rose comes over with Roman sometimes and so does Kara. Rose brings some of her oils over and uses them on him daily and he does seem to relax and be a bit more aware after she has used them. She leaves some with me to use every couple of hours, another day of that and he is groggy but aware.

This morning, he wakens me with a soft kiss on my cheek next to him. He says his head hurts too much to raise it up for a decent kiss.

Hey, I am happy to have any kiss from him right now. I check his eyes and have him track my finger. He is very woozy when we go for the standing up part of the test, but he makes it without collapsing. That's a plus.

I help him get dressed and he is sitting on the couch when his Dad walks in. Roman's face lights up like he just got exactly what he wanted for Christmas when he was a child. This is even better, his child is awake and talking.

I fix some soup and crackers for him to have something semi-solid on his stomach. He has lost weight while out and I want to fatten him up. At least enough to lose the gaunt look he has. He never had much extra to lose, anyway.

Now that he is up, he wants to get right back to work, but finds he is a lot weaker than he expected to be. Several days unconscious does that to a person. No food or water for that time, does also. I managed to spoon small amounts of liquids down him, but was afraid I would get fluid in his lungs and make a bad situation even worse.

The first couple of days is mainly getting him rehydrated. I make broths using meat base with lots of vegetables added, then strained, for him to drink. I vary the seasonings so it isn't always just the same flavor. Elaine always wants a cup to share with Daddy, so she gets some, too.

About the time he is getting able to resume working, I have a miscarriage. I didn't even know for sure that I was with child. This really knocks me for a loop. I guess I thought I was invincible or something, but I have never had to deal with something like this. I cry most of the night and Noah holds me and comforts me. Somehow now that it is gone, I feel like I have missed something precious and of value in my life.

I don't want to get up the next morning, and stay with my head under the covers for as long as possible. However, there is a small human that depends on me and doesn't know she has lost a sibling. She is tiptoeing in ever couple of minutes to check on Mom. I have to quit dwelling on myself and take care of the treasures I do have, Elaine and Noah.

Somehow, I feel fragile. I never have been and am built too sturdy to actually look fragile, but that is how I feel. I ease back into working as we need all the chores done every day, no matter what. Noah and I are quite a pair, both recuperating and working as much as we can.

Chapter 18

We must be getting more organized or better at our jobs. Winter has arrived and all the hay is harvested, the grain and straw is, also. The gardens are all taken care of and most of the greenhouses are heated and still producing. We finished construction, finally, on our second larger heated greenhouse and have the beds ready to plant early next spring.

I never asked what happened to the prisoner and I don't think I want to know. Everyone is trying to pay better attention now in case more of them show up from his camp. If they all feel like he does, we probably should just go wipe them out, but that seems a bit too cold blooded, even to me.

Before cold weather set in, Liz and Richard and some of their group took a pack train of horses loaded with trade supplies in to town. They wanted to open trade with people in Fairbanks and North Pole area and see old friends. They expected to be gone about 2 weeks and they made it home in just 2 days over.

They had a great time and visited with several old friends from visits in years past. The cattle, horses, chickens and turkeys they left are thriving and multiplying very well.

They didn't make it farther out to see how the group near the military base was doing, but the North Pole group was in touch and said they were doing very well, also. They were trading grain and some other supplies back and forth.

Word had even filtered in from Delta and things were going well out there, also. The school was expanding and they were trying to convince a teacher to move out from Fairbanks to just teach, instead of parents taking turns.

Sara's daughter, Tina is now talking just like any other little girl her age. So whatever trauma had made her mute for so long evidently was overcome by everyone just letting her be a little girl and loving her.

Sara and Isaiah, one of the young men from Canada, got married just before winter. They moved to one of the cabin sites along the road between Jeremy and Rose. We all helped build a nice cabin for them and woodshed, then helped fill the woodshed.

By the time the winter holidays came around, everyone was settled in and doing well. Noah and I were both recovered and feeling good again. We both seemed to have observed the happenings between his injury and the holidays as through a fog. We functioned, but we certainly were not at our best.

By the middle of November, we harvested the last of our produce from the heated greenhouse and allowed it to freeze up. Our total produce production from it was amazing and we definitely managed to save seeds on the varieties we grew in it. We dried and packaged them up to share around the neighborhood so everyone could grow more, next season and not all be dependant on our keeping them viable.

I set a few snares out and about, just in case more wolves moved into our area. At the moment, it seemed fairly wolf free. I don't want to have to keep after them, but I also don't want to lose our means of staying alive to them, either.

We all barely made it on the amount of dried fish we had on hand for the dogs. If it had been a worse winter, we would have been short supplies. As it is, they are getting short rations by the time we can start catching fish again.

The following spring, just after we finish the birch sap gathering and before the ice has gone out on the rivers, we make one last trip up to the Yukon river with the old pickup.

When we stop on the Pump Station side, we see people around the buildings on the other side, so honk the pickup horn and yell over to them. They stare at us as though we dropped from another planet.

Noah walks halfway down the old cracked bridge to the center and one of them walks up to meet him. I carefully keep them covered from my perch with Elaine by the pickup, without allowing the gun to show.

They talk for quite a while, then Noah turns and walks back toward me. This is a family that used to live a bit farther up the river and they floated down to see if they could use this cleared area to start a farm on. He has offered them chickens, a couple of turkeys and maybe a couple of goats to start and when they have better accommodations for them, a few cows in the future if they want.

They can't believe it and accept immediately. We will give one a ride back with us and pick up some stuff and bring back the chickens, goats and at least fertile turkey eggs. I have several hens going broody, so they can have a couple of them to start their flock.

We don't feel right taking stuff they might need in the future so we don't salvage any more from the Pump Station. We just give the guy a ride to our place. Thad will ride back with Noah to deliver the animals.

We have a pregnant nanny and a young billy goat that we send back with instructions on care and how long until her birth and milking directions. Same with the chickens. They fuel up the pickup and take the man and animals back to the bridge.

As they are unloading, a couple of kids bring up some bundles to give Noah in exchange. They did very well trapping over the winter and have tanned the furs to a lovely soft hide and fur. We now have several really nice beaver pelts. These are excellent for mitts and trapper hats that wear a very long time and are very warm. What a great trade.

I included some packets of seed to grow a garden as the Yukon valley is very good for agriculture. Maybe we can get more gardens and farms going up here and everyone enjoy a pretty good standard of living instead of just surviving.

There are some feral hogs around Delta, but we don't want to get those started in our area. Not only are they destructive of gardens and grain fields, they are dangerous to humans, also. We have enough danger without adding some on purpose.

Al thought he might like to get some, but after thinking it over, decided he really didn't want the hassle. Now if he could manage to capture a few of the bison calves, those, he would love to get started here.

He decided to drive up to the bridge to show the folks there where his boat and nets are stashed so they can net salmon this summer. They are thrilled to meet him and use his supplies.

We have let our caribou loose. We have quite a nice small herd of them, but we don't need them now. Maybe they will stay around in our valley, maybe they won't, but we did get to use them before the cattle herd showed up. They were nice in harness, also.

We are surprised later in the year to find that part of the White Mountain herd have joined our little herd. Maybe getting rid of a lot of their predators helped them decide.

Shari's second child is a little girl. She named her Georgia, to go with Savannah, her first daughter. Having moved up here from there, she has fond memories of the area.

We have quite a few children running around the community now and it is about time to start some type of school for them.

Liz home schooled her girls and one granddaughter. Kara home schooled her teens. The rest of us have no experience at all. Rose draws up some books for beginner reading. She paints the pages on cloth and stitches the books together. They should last a while.

Shari is willing to give it a try, teaching all

the assorted children. She is firm but not mean about them minding, and they all love her. Elaine picks up a soft southern drawl in her reading. Now if she picks up some better manners to go along with it….. We have been lax on social skill's, I guess.

It's not like we are suddenly going to be attending any actual social functions, but she should have some manners in public. She does have pretty good table manners. She has a good eye with her slingshot and can milk a goat. She can sneak up on a grouse and grab it by hand. The girl has some skills.

Al takes Walter to school by dog sled so he stops and picks up Elaine on his way by and drops her off every evening. I am not used to having her gone at all, so I am just a little bit lost while she is gone, the first couple of days. Then it is woo-hoo, I have some time on my hands.

Noah and I take full advantage of our time alone. We read books. Uninterrupted reading time is rare around here. Ha, you thought I was going to say something else, didn't you?

School will only be through the middle of winter, as the children have to help around home the rest of the time. Growing up working, they will always know how. Shari has too much to do, herself, to teach any other time of the year. Gardening, and caring for the animals and children, while Will gets the firewood and does the haying.

Each family with children wants the child to grow up knowing how to survive. If something happened and they were left alone, they would need to know.

Chapter 19

There is evidence that more of the people from Amy's friends are still hanging around. Several of our men want to go hunt them down. Never knowing if someone is going to attack while you are working or steal what you have just worked to accomplish wears on the nerves after a while. After Noah's injuries, I tend to agree with hunting them down.

We should have. They have raided again and this time there are casualties. They burned the cabin with everyone in it, over on one of the small parcels settled by some of the young adults. From the remaining evidence, they first stripped the house and the people were bound when the cabin was burned. Now it is our own small war.

Dan checks over his plane, he is our Air Force. Thad is our Army and Jeremy, the Marine Corp. They make some small bombs from supplies taken from the tractor/trailer and the camp we took out earlier.

The trail through the snow shows very well. Did they think no one was going to retaliate? Are they planning an ambush of the plane?

Dan flies in high over the area they seem to be holed up in. He circled wide out of rifle range before coming in closer. Thad and Jeremy are prepared and toss the bombs out as soon as they are over the camp. There is the ping of a bullet hitting the ski on one side of the plane so they are shooting back, until the bombs go off. Dan flies over again and the second drop of bombs is made. Dan lands and Jeremy has the small rocket launcher and uses one into the middle of the camp area.

As long as they have been here, they could have built cabins and lived in comfort instead of still camping in makeshift shelters. The area looks like it would be perfect for a settlement and has enough browse and fairly flat ground for nice fields. They are just too set in taking what they want to learn to do it themselves. What a waste of people.

They go in search and destroy mode. None of them wants to deal with this group ever again. The air attack has taken care of it for them. There is no one left to destroy.

While flying home, Dan looks the terrain over and likes the area better than where he is living right now. If Melanie is up to it, he wants to move over here and build himself a larger place.

Summer, it might look a lot different, but he will come check it out, then. Thad likes it too, and will come with him.

There is a collective sigh of relief when they return home, safe. There are a couple more bullet holes in the plane but nothing important was hit and Dan patches the plane easily. The weapons they picked up around camp are stored in case they are needed in the future. There was some ammunition, but not much.

Dan can't wait until Summer to go check that area out. He and Thad decide on a winter camping trip and maybe a bit of scouting. They go from the end of the road made to Liz and Richard's property on up over that hill. It is almost directly beyond the area already cleared. It's a good thing no one in that group had a topo map of the area, they were almost directly behind Liz's house. Instead, they always walked around the end of the hill and up from the river.

The small valley is nice and gentle sloped, facing almost directly south. The view across the main valley it opens onto is toward the Alaska Range of mountains and is breath taking. It would be open to more wind, but it is a lovely valley.

Melanie isn't too sure about moving over there, but agrees they should go ahead and clear the fields and build barns, develop it into a place and then she and Patricia would move over, when the house is done. Dan asked her what did she think, he was going to expect her to move over right now and live in a tent? Gee, that went well.

By the time spring finally gets here, several of the young adults at Rose's place want to go check out that valley for possible places for themselves. They have learned how to live out here, now and are confident they can make their own places just as well as the ones we have already done.

By spring, the men have cleared large areas to start building. Each one has staked out a good large area of the gently sloping hillsides, bordering what they hope is a nice creek.

Rose agrees to bring her dozer over and do the fields, so they don't have the stumps to contend with. The trip over and back will make a road for them.

That was the plan and the first two parts of it worked very well. On the trip back, not so much.

Two weeks worth of thawing while clearing the fields thawed enough of the proposed roadbed that the dozer sunk, clear to the frame.

The good news was, if they dig this area out, after the dozer is out of it, they will probably have a good strong spring for more water.

The bad news is, that usually it takes a larger dozer to pull a stuck dozer out. Since that was not an option, volunteers were asked to come dig. Trees were fell all around the area to use fastened across the tracks to try breaking the suction and lift the dozer enough to stuff more logs in under it and build up firm enough footing under the dozer to walk itself out. Sounds simple, doesn't it?

The sheer volume of logs needed was staggering. If there was a way of salvaging the logs after the dozer is out, this would be enough firewood for several homes for the winter.

Rose uses the hydraulics to push the front as far up in the air as possible with the blade and logs are stuffed in under it. The blade is raised and a couple of logs are chained across the tracks then the dozer is put in gear and inches it's way up onto the logs under it as more are thrown in front of it.

When the chained logs come around to the back, they have to be undone and more logs chained across the front after raising and filling in again. Eventually the dozer pulls it's way clear of the mud sucking it down. Once she is far enough away to stop, without worry about starting to sink again, it is time to clean the heavy mud off the tracks and under-carriage.

Everyone is a mucky mess by the time Rose has the dozer headed home again. She carefully cut a path around above the area

now looking like a bog hole. That would not
be such a great road for quite a while. Maybe
a small lake as it thaws more.

The men start right away on their hauling
supplies over. The road will only get worse
for a while and they want everything needed
in place before they can't drive it any more
this spring.

Dan wants to place his barns so the south
wall is able to be used to espalier his apple
trees against it. Any other buildings will be
placed with that in mind, also.

Thad doesn't want to live over there, he just
wants to start a farm of some sort to work
on. He wants to raise some cattle and maybe
a horse or two, but mostly, he wants to grow
stuff. Grain, hay, gardens, even just large
potato fields, he just enjoys growing useful
things. He wants to place his barn and
outbuildings fairly close to Dan's, so if Dan
wants, he can plant espaliered trees along his
walls, also. That is one way of growing fruit
crops in borderline areas of survival for the
trees. It looks odd, it works.

My little trees I have planted against the
house and barn are doing quite well. I feel
bad trimming off any branches wanting to
grow out, but the trained ones against the
walls are shaping up nicely and so far the
moose have not gotten any of them. Some
even look like they may bloom this season.

Chapter 20

We were so wrong. Royal is not dead. He is sitting in my living room holding Elaine and she is not a happy little girl. His face is a horror. The scar tissue from freezing covers most of his face and pulls his mouth into a sneering grin. Most of his nose and ears are gone, so are most of his eyelids. His hands are claws. He is skinny as a rail and with his lips mostly gone, he drools and it makes him even worse tempered.

When he came walking into my kitchen carrying Elaine from her bedroom, I just about passed out. He must have come in through a window.

This is worse than any of the horror shows my Mom used to drag us to, when I was a kid. She loved them, I hated them. I hate this, even more.

He is hard to understand, but the evil glares out at me. He laughs at how we all thought that other body was him. That was the kind person that gave him a ride out here from town and then his parka, only that wasn't willingly. He killed him for the parka and left him lay beside the snow machine.

He is demanding I bring him Shari. He blames her for all the bad choices he and his sons made and are still making. I can't bring him Shari to murder, and I can't leave him with my little girl.

His mind is so twisted, who knows what he will do to her if I am not here? He takes the decision out of my hands by pushing me out the door and locking it behind me. Now he is in my house holding my daughter hostage.

Noah is over helping Thad. So is Roman. Jeremy and Dan are working on Dan's place. Will and Shari have taken their 3 children to visit Steve and Dani about 20 miles north of us and plan on spending the weekend there. I head for Rose and Kara.

They are both home and they get me settled down enough to talk. They are horrified to hear what has just happened. We try to think of what we can do and nothing seems possible. I don't know how much time I have before he loses what patience he has and hurts or kills my daughter. We think of all kinds of things but nothing sounds like it can possibly work.

We finally decide on just having him think he is getting what he wants. Rose is a little taller than Shari, but that is only noticeable if they stand side by side. Shari don't weigh as much, but loose fitting clothing and he has not seen Shari in years, so she might have gained weight, should pass.

Rose wears an old outfit with a hood that covers her head and face pretty well so he can't tell who is coming in the drive with me. Kara will sneak around from the other side and come in through the chicken coop. All the chickens are out in their mobile coop between rows in the garden so won't give her away.

Rose is wearing body armor under the hoodie. I just hope he doesn't do something the armor doesn't cover. She also has some of her potions and dried supplies with her to make tea.

When I tap on the door, Royal opens it right away. He still has Elaine pulled against his body as a shield and she has her eyes open, but he covered her mouth with tape to keep her quiet. Her hands are not bound, so she reaches for me. He yanks her back and Rose and I both come into the room. Rose hangs back behind me, acting the shy, scared little woman Shari used to be.

She whispers that she can make us all a good cup of tea, and scurries over to my stove. I have hot water on the heater and she takes the kettle as she goes.

Royal looks pleased to have her waiting on

him. She brews up 1 cup of tea and sets it on
the table while backing up. He tells her to
make some for all of us as we have some
talking to do, so she makes us each a cup. I
notice ours is out of a different container
than his. His has mint in it also, for the odor,
but ours is only mint.

He sits down and motions us to do so, too.
He never lets go of Elaine. She looks like she
is about to explode and I can almost see little
wheels turning in her head. She is surprised
to see us afraid of this awful man.

He sips his tea as he glares at us, and seems
to like the flavor, so takes larger sips. It is
slightly acidic but the mint helps cover that
and the birch syrup sweetener. His mouth
must be damaged from the freezing so he
doesn't notice the burning sensation from the
baneberries. Maybe he thinks that is from the
tea being so hot. Rose and I sip at ours also.
He is getting aggravated that she still has the
hood over her head and says something about
her bad manners and that he will soon have
that knocked out of her.

His stomach must be giving him some
problems as he starts squirming around a bit,
trying to get comfortable. Rose left the lid
off the kettle of hot water and has it close to
her hand, as he starts to comprehend what is
happening, she throws it at him, almost
missing, trying not to hit Elaine.

I have already jumped forward and grabbed Elaine away from his twitching fingers before he can hurt her any more than he already has. Rose grabs the hand he has a gun in, and forces it back and he pulls the trigger, hitting the wall right beside Elaine's head.

Kara is in the door right behind him, smacking his ears or where his ears should be. Then smashing a hammer into his skull. Between the tea and the hammer, I don't think we have to worry about Royal any more.

I am hugging and kissing my poor little girl as we gently take the tape off her little mouth and checking her all over. She has some bruising, but looks okay. She is patient but as soon as the tape is gone, she walks over and kicks him for good measure.

We drag his sorry carcass outside and sit around on the steps, trying to get our nerves back in a calmer mode. Kara and I help Rose get the body armor off. We don't even know if we got it on her correctly. I am a wreck. I want to cry, but not sure why, now that it is already over.

Kara is surprised that she actually sunk a hammer into someone's head. Rose tells her not to feel bad, he was already a dead man, just didn't know it yet, he drank enough baneberry tea to kill a horse. Kara says she doesn't feel bad, he needed killing, it was just not something she expected to do. She wasn't wanting to use her gun and maybe hit one of us.

We drag him on over to the edge of my yard. I don't know what to do with him and although he has lost a lot of weight, he is still a large man. Being summer, we can't just leave him lay, he will start smelling soon and I really don't want that in my yard.

We finally decide it is worth using the fuel and load him in the back of my pickup. All 4 of us get in after locking up the house, and the door into the coop. We might as well show Shari and Will that the problem is finally truly over.

We drive up to Steve and Dani's place and they are all standing outside wondering who has enough fuel to be out driving around. I motion Will over and he comes to the pickup. I point in back and he takes a look, then another look. Steve comes over and the women keep the kids back. This isn't something any of them need to see and I am sure Elaine will have nightmares from it for a while.

We ask the guys what we can do with him. No one has any good ideas, other than just drop him off along the road somewhere between here and home, preferably over a large drop off.

Will looks relieved to finally see proof that Royal will not ever show up again. Shari will be, once she knows.

On our way home, we stop at a steep bank down to the river and push our load off over the bank. No one lives around here and he shouldn't bother anyone.

I take Rose and Kara home. Then Elaine and I go home and check out the house and lock all the doors. We aren't feeling really secure right at the moment. I nailed a piece of plywood over the window Royal took out to gain access to the house. He stayed so quite, even our dogs hadn't noticed.

When Noah gets home that evening, Elaine is the first one to tell him about our day. She acted out the hammer to the head ending very well.

He grabs her and checks her all over while his beautiful eyes ask me a million questions. Once he is satisfied she is really okay, he holds her and pulls me into their embrace. Elaine has had enough of being held today and wiggles to be let down. The lavender oil we put on her bruises has most of them fading already. The bruises are fading but the memories may linger a long time. I know I am going to see that face in my nightmares for quite a while.

We remain jumpy and Elaine and I both start having nightmares. Finally she tells me she just kicked him again and he would never come back. Somehow that seemed to fix her nightmares. Mine lasted longer.

Since we don't know how much longer the gas is going to be stable, we decide to drive back up to the Yukon and check on the folks up there. We have got in the habit of pulling the trailer along whenever we go anywhere, just in case. We park on the south side of the bridge and walk over.

Xander, Avanell and kids, Perry, Rhonda and Simon are happy to see friendly faces again. Xander has got one of the old pickups running that was out back and pumped up gas from the underground tanks. Then he used it as a tractor and they have cleared and planted several acres to grass for hay. They planted the grain we gave them along one side to hand harvest and save seed from.

They gave up on making any of the old motel livable and are expanding the little cabin Amy and Natalie spent the winter in. The wood stove is a very good one so should be fine. They took off the roof, made a second story and put the roof back on.

They are keeping the large workshop to use as a barn and will tear down most of the other buildings for the materials in them. All the windows will make a great greenhouse for them. We tell them about heating ours with the mass heater and show them how to construct one for theirs. They are going to use the shop as one wall and place the greenhouse against the south side of it.

Since the shop is insulated, they should have a great greenhouse that way. They are saving all the insulation from the motel and café as they dismantle them but don't want to try storing it. They offer us some of it and we accept.

We turn our pickup around and back it and the trailer to the edge of the bridge. Then we start loading insulation on a little wagon and pulling it across the bridge to load the trailer and pickup. It will be a light load, but it will take up a lot of room. I want to use part to insulate our barn better.

By the time we can't find another way to keep any more on our load, we look like a bad cartoon of squatters.

We leave the bag of baking supplies we brought for them and head on home. I'm hoping Hess Creek bridge really is safe to cross. It looked okay when we checked it on our way up. I never know whether to ease across or step on it and go as fast as possible across a questionable bridge. I really prefer going around. We drive carefully across it. We stop at Steve and Dani's and see how they are getting along. Then directly to the house.

We unload as much of the insulation as we think we will need in the near future and haul the rest down to Roman. He has the large building he was going to use to sell building supplies out here, before the quake. This will give him some stock plus keep it dry.

We start insulating the barn roof with this insulation the next day. After we get that done, we add a good vapor barrier. This should be far more comfortable for the animals in winter. I might not have to blanket the little ones all winter. While we are at it, we insulate the rest of the walls better and add vapor barrier. This should be a comfy barn from now on.

We have shutters, inside and outside both, so we can close it up from either side. The inside shutters have a sheet of foam board between 2 sheets of metal to insulate and be harder to gain entry through. The outer shutters are just metal. With the lower walls being rock, the building should be fairly safe from forest fires. The doors are the weak link. If we ever make it back to the Yukon, I should ask about making a deal on the metal clad doors they have for some of the out-buildings. They should be at least fire resistant. Maybe I should ask Roman if he has metal sheets enough to build me a couple.

He not only does but will. He comes over and measures the door areas the very next day. He brings them over on his pony cart a few days later and installs them. They are beautiful and he welded on designs to make them even prettier. They can be latched from the inside and the drawstring pulled in so no one can open them from the outside. Then he shows me how to over ride that in case one of the children locks themselves in the barn.

Chapter 21

We are going to see if we can drive to Manley. There are only a few bridges and we can check those out. If they are damaged, we can probably drive around them in the streams as it has not started raining yet.

I load up some cheeses and a couple of the young goats and we head out. We have the trailer behind, just in case we see something we really need and can get. Roman has built nice sides on it, so it can haul almost anything.

Rose asked if we managed to get as far as Eureka, to turn and go to her old mining cabin and recover anything of use, there. She drew us a map and wrote out directions and showed us some photos, so we would know we had the right place.

We stop first at the family on the Hutlinana and they want the goats as they now have a small barn built and hay cut and stored in it for winter. We leave the goats with them. The little nanny will give birth in a month or so, and the billy isn't a sibling, he is from the other nanny we have. I give them some of the cheese and the recipe.

We found her cabin okay and it had been pretty well stripped. But no one looked out in the brush on the other side of the road and there was an old dump bed from a truck filled entirely with assorted metal. We also loaded all the metal concrete forms that were left. As we searched around, we found a lot of things to take back to her, including canning jars stashed under one of the trailer houses.

We find some of her mint plants and Viola flowers volunteering near the front door and dig some up to take to her. She has so many memories of her time out here, maybe it will bring back some more of them.

We stop at the Baker Creek bridge. It appears to be too damaged to drive over. We visit a while with the folks living near the bridge and the cattle and chickens they got from Liz and Richard are doing very well. I give them some cheese and the recipe. Cows' milk will be a bit different, but they can experiment. They give us some tomatoes they picked up at the greenhouses in Manley the day before. They plan on going back tomorrow and can get more.

We head for home. When we get to Ptarmigan Pass, the fog has lifted that covered the valley below when we came by this morning. We pull over to look out over the whole valley and it looks more like a huge lake. This has been a dry year, so it can't be from flooding. It looks like the entire Tanana Valley has sunk and the water levels are very high. There is no sign of the village that used to be visible from here. When our men took the boat out into the valley, they said the water tasted brackish, so maybe we do have some ocean water coming this far up. If we hear seals barking along the river some day, we will start looking for whales. I guess it could be possible.

On the low hills that used to be above the village, there is evidence of some clearing and smoke, so maybe some of the villagers escaped and made it through the years since.

With the rivers now being so much wider, most of the villages along them all the way to the Bering Sea must have flooded out during the quake. The people that left Natalie at the Yukon may not have found a better life downstream. By the time they realized this, they would not have enough fuel remaining to come back to the road system. All the villages I have seen along the river are right along the banks.

We took our load of metal on down to dump at Rose's place. We off load on the upper drive so it won't be in the way and is handy for Roman when he needs to fabricate anything. We leave his trailer there, also. Then we take the plants down to Rose from her old cabin. She thanks us and is looking for an area to plant them right away.

We drive home and thoroughly enjoy what may be one of the last trips we ever get to make. Well, we can always go by horse or dog team. Somehow it isn't the same. We unload the rest of the tomatoes here at home and I will start canning them tomorrow.

We are all starting to relax again. Maybe this time, we actually can, without some horrible thing or people coming along. It's just been one thing after another and I am tired of it. We have cleared a lot of vermin out of the gene pool. I would like to think we had good reason for each and every one of them.

The only one I still have nightmares about, is Royal. That was the scariest man I have ever met or seen. I almost want to stop where we dropped him over the bank to make sure he is still down there.

Epilogue:
Ten years later.

I think we can say most of the kinks have been worked out of our current civilization. There isn't much to it, it is similar to civilization before the Industrial Revolution back two or three hundred years ago without the kings and politicians. So it's not all bad.

We still have the knowledge but no means of using the knowledge, for electronics, mechanization and fuel distillation.. Within 2 generations, no one will remember any of it. We are trying to keep our children taught how to read and do math and study all the how-to books everyone has on hand. Roman, Richard and Mike have the young men disassemble and reassemble the gas and diesel motors for the dozer, backhoe and loader, then the tractors working with the wood gasifiers.

We have used up almost all of the supplies we had or acquired during the years immediately following The Earthquake. We have had other earthquakes, but the one that destroyed everything we knew has attained capitalization status.

Oh, some of us still have some spices in

stock and use them sparingly. Salt has become a major trade item, with folks along the coast having a lucrative business going in sea salt production.

The day a sailing ship pulled into the harbor near Wasilla, and was loaded with trade items from the tropics was a major breakthrough in international trading. They also brought rats and some illnesses with them and for a while, it was doubtful if there were going to be many survivors from that, south of the Alaska Range. Since then, folks are leery about commerce with outsiders coming in on ships.

We only heard about it a couple of years later after a trading trek with horses and wagons went to Fairbanks. We trade a lot with the folks around Manley and some north at the Yukon Bridge. The people at Delta have regular travel by horse in summer and dogs in winter, to Fairbanks and once in a while down to Haines Junction, in Canada. We still call these places by the names we are used to or the ones they had before. No one seems to want to change them and it is rather comforting to know some places have been there a while.

People have died, and more have been born. We have a fairly large community here although it is still scattered out fairly well. Most of the people that thought they could steal for a living have met sudden deaths. It is not a habit that endeared them to anyone and no one wanted to house and feed them in a prison of any sort. We have neither the resources nor the want, to even attempt that. Some of us older ones refer to lazy thieves as Amys. The younger ones just look at us like we are silly old folks.

Roman and Rose never have got married. They each continued to keep each other company most of the time and kept their own homes. Thad and Kara did the same. Thad's farm project is a great success. He usually plants most of his fields to potatoes. Then grain around the sides and the next year, grain in the middle and potatoes around the sides. He does vary this with other crops now and then.

Liz and Richard have their family group all settled around them in their own homes. Their friends and the folks that moved up from Canada are doing well, also. The gunsmith has made some lovely guns for anyone having the materials and ammo. He is excellent at making parts for equipment, also.

Dan and Melanie have 2 children and they are getting along very well indeed. There children are well behaved and helpful. Nice kids.

Jeremy and Ashley have 3 children and they also still have Joey living with them. Joey is so sweet natured, everyone loves him and all the children watch over him like protective little mother hens. He, on the other hand, has saved several of the children when we were raided one time by a group trying to steal children and raise them as slaves.

Then our retired military came out of retirement and hunted them down and that has not been a problem again. Most of their captives were from Fairbanks, so they were returned home. The ones with no homes left to return to, were welcomed into our community.

Al and Natalie have 4 children now and Farren is still with them. He is the older brother or uncle to all the kids and is very good with them.

Steve and Dani have Boys 1, 2, 3, and 4. Girl 1 showed up last and is everyone's little pet. Boy 1 thinks he might like to be called Adam, but he hasn't fully decided yet. Boy 2 says no way is he going to be Cain or Able.

Joel and Annie got married and have a few children. They always seem to have others visiting, so it is hard to figure out just which ones and how many are theirs.

Xander and Avanell from the Yukon Bridge have had a couple more children. Their daughter Rhonda married Leif that came up from Canada with Liz and Richard. He moved up there and built a home for his family. They have really made a lovely farm out of the whole area. It is still easiest to cross on the ice if we want to travel up to see them or walk across the remains of the bridge. The bridge is getting less stable, so I don't like walking on it at all.

Noah and I have 2 more children. I didn't think I would or could. Never have found many maternal bones in this body, but the children are growing and thriving and not all that bad to have around. We named our first son James Roman after his Grandfather, just switching the names around. Our second son was harder to name. Noah's middle name is Avery, he hates it and neither of us wanted the boy to be called Avery. It is a nice name, just didn't sound right for this boy.

We were taking so long to name him, everyone thought we would end up like Steve and Dani and just call him Boy. Rose came over one day and said call him Charlie. So now he is Charles Noah.

Those names don't exactly roll off the tongue when said together, but he is named for good men. He has a great curiosity about how things are put together. Rose says yes, he really is a Charlie. She said Charlie could take apart and repair anything at all, whether he had ever seen the item before or not. Whether it was an electronic something clear up to a giant crane he reassembled on one of the old D.E.W. line sites. Give him a little time and he could fly a plane even. Maybe our Charlie will be that way, too.

20 years after that:

It's hard to believe, we are now considered the some of the old wise ones. Roman and Rose have both died, by accident. They were working with a distillery process they came up with to make some fuel for the old gas vehicles still sitting around as yard ornaments. I'm so not ready to be a Village Elder.

My children have children. Even worse, some of them are having children, also. That is the hardest part to keep in mind. I still feel like a young woman. I am sure glad I don't have many mirrors around so I don't get a scare wondering who that old woman is staring back at me.

When I look at Noah, I still see the beautiful melted chocolate eyes and his gorgeous smile. Maybe eyes going bad is a good thing, he can't see how old I am, either. He truly has been the very best husband I could ever have asked for. Even if I wasn't even looking, when he showed up. I've noticed a lot of my better moments were not planned.

Will and Shari are doing fairly well. Shari fell a while back and hurt her hip. Will carries her around and she says he is ruining his back and she can't carry him when it goes. They also have grandchildren and great-grandchildren.

Richard and Liz are actually the Elders of the whole valley. When anyone wants to know exactly what is needed, they still go to them. Liz will be 100 on her next birthday. She wants to go riding, and probably will.

There are too many to mention on children and great-grandchildren. We have been fruitful and multiplied, that is for sure.

The inland sea has moderated our climate a little bit. More snow and less cold, I don't mind that. The fruit trees and berries Dan flew in have grown well and produce. Liz showed everyone how to make starts from the trees, so everyone has fruit trees now. Apples, plums and cherries, which most of us thought we would never get to eat again.

The cattle Liz and Richard brought up from Oregon and along the way have made the whole area around us cattle country. There is enough Highlander crossed in all of them now that they grow a good winter coat.

We brush all the animals to gather fiber to spin and knit or weave. Some of it works far better than others. The dogs in the spring actually have a nice bunch of fleece to brush out. It gives different colors and nice hats, mittens and socks.

We do make some felt from some of the hair gathered. The boots and boot liners are nice from that. Even hat liners can be made from it.

The horses are mostly fairly sturdy stock. They also have a good winter coat that gets brushed and saved. Everything has a use, sometimes we just take a while to find out what it is.

Manley has managed to renew trade with Fairbanks by boat. The greenhouses supply fresh produce year around. We have built a dock near the mouth of our little river and we sometimes get some produce from them, but we manage to grow almost everything we need. Our mass heaters in our greenhouses help out very much.

Chena Hot Springs didn't fare too well, a lot of their hot water disappeared in the quake and they never were able to get back to the degree of self sufficiency they had in the past.

We have not heard anything from the Circle Hot Spring area. There used to be a group near there that had some definitely non Christian habits and I think sometime in the future, they could be a problem if they survived the quake. Their women were seldom seen and always totally covered in black. I'm just glad they are a long ways from us. I wish it were farther.

Fairbanks has rebuilt on a much smaller scale. Downtown was left alone to start with, then used as salvage, with most rebuilding done in the hills north of town. Most of the windows that were still whole, have been salvaged and most used for greenhouses. Food takes priority over homes having lots of windows. The areas level enough for fields are kept as fields for growing food and hay or grain.

The cattle have been bred for milking, mostly. So they are getting more milk now from their cattle. They also have a thriving cheese making business there.

North Pole is doing fine. There are several small farms all around the area and they are a hard working bunch.

Delta is doing great. They may end up becoming the main source of food for the whole territory.

We hear word now and then that some folks are trying to organize a government again. They didn't do so well last time, why not just leave it be?

We still consider ourselves Alaskan, but most of us feel like we are our own country now, lets not muck it up.

The community down at Haines Junction is growing and thriving. They are exporting by horse drawn wagons to other areas near them to the south.

The farm down near Smithers has become a major growing area for that part of B.C.

The Okanogan Valley area is doing extremely well, with all the fruits no one farther north can grow. They mainly dehydrate and ship as dried fruits, but it is better than none at all.

Most of the shipping in the north is done by dog team now. The roads are terrible and none of the bridges have been repaired, except very small spans near a community that is starting to thrive.

There never were many roads in Alaska, so the old trails work just fine and new ones were made where the old ones disappeared. Boats are used quite a bit, in summer. But they have to be people powered, so that limits how far anyone is willing to travel. The wind helps some on sails a few people have set up on their boats, if they can wait for it to be blowing or in the right direction.

For Alaska, this has not been as far a step back into the past for survival. When it happened, there were still people alive and living here that remembered how it used to be.

The people that survived in the villages went back to the nomadic life they had lived before the Alaska Native Lands Settlement put them all in villages established in what was usually old fish camps, gold rush settlements or even Russian fur trade settlements.

It was far easier to move the whole camp to a dead moose than it was to move the dead moose to a camp, so camps were mobile and didn't overuse the land in the area they were established in. The next kill moved the camp to the next location. Very practical.

Summer fish camps were fairly well established for each group. So later, those were used as the foundation for the permanent villages required by the government.

Government really likes to have everyone stuck in densely populated areas to keep track of all they are doing. I guess that makes sense if the government doesn't trust the people or the people can't trust their government.

I see my dear Love coming in the driveway. I better heat up the stew and make sure the water is hot for a shower. I have plans for him, tonight. I traded for some new books, or at least new for us. We will have a quiet evening reading by the fire.

Earth Battery, (thanks to Wilderness Joe)
Drive alternating copper & galvanized rods
about 2' deep & about 2' apart into
the ground. Connect all of those rods
together with electrical wire. Use 1 of
those cheap electric multi meters to see when
you reach 12 volts, check the
amperage as well. To get more amps. run
more sets in parallel until you get
enough power. An inverter can easily turn this
12 volt source into regular 110
volt AC. One end of the wire will be - the
other end will be +.
From Mark : Zinc, the lovely metal on the
outside of galvanized steel, is relatively
reactive and prone to oxidation, and would
corrode easily but for the fact
that a thin layer of zinc oxide protects the
metal. (The same principle
protects aluminum, which is also reactive.) In
a wet environment, zinc
corrodes more easily, and the process
generates a little electric current.
So, if you put a galvanized rod into ground,
and another rod of less

reactive (more noble) metal to complete a circuit through the soil, then
you could get a small current. (If you don't have a copper-clad rod, gold
or platinum would work just fine.) An earth battery is just a variation of
the ordinary dry cell battery, which also oxidizes metallic zinc to make
power. But D cells are far easier to use, and they can be stacked in
series to add more voltage, whereas an earth battery cannot, because all of
the copper rods are "grounded". Adding more rods will increase current.
When the zinc is all oxidized, then the earth battery will be nearly dead.
Iron is more reactive than copper, and will generate a tiny voltage

The following recipes are from my cookbook, **"Don't Use A Chainsaw In The Kitchen".** **Volume 2**

POTSTICKERS

Potstickers are one of the most popular types of Chinese dumplings. This recipe includes a dipping sauce and instructions on making the dough.

Yields about 48 potstickers.
Ingredients:
- Dumpling Dough*
- 2 cups all purpose flour
- 1 cup boiling water
- Filling:
- 8 ounces celery cabbage (Napa cabbage)regular cabbage is fine
- 3 tsp salt, divided
- 1 pound lean ground pork, chicken or beef (any meat will do, or none at all)
- 1/4 cup finely chopped green onions, with tops
- 1 tsp cornstarch

- 1 tsp sesame oil
- Dash white pepper (black pepper works fine)
- Dipping Sauce:
- 1/4 cup soy sauce
- 1 tsp sesame oil (optional)
- Other:
- 2 - 4 tablespoons seasoned vinegar

Preparation:

Cut the cabbage across into thin strips. Mix with 2 teaspoons salt and set aside for 5 minutes. Squeeze out the excess moisture.

In a large bowl, mix the celery cabbage, meat, green onions, cornstarch, the remaining 1 teaspoon salt, 1 teaspoon sesame oil, and the white pepper.

Dough:

In a bowl, mix the flour and 1 cup boiling water until a soft dough forms. Knead the dough on a lightly flour surface about 5 minutes, or until smooth.

Divide the dough in half. Shape each half into a roll 12 inches long and cut each roll into 1/2-inch slices.

Roll 1 slice of dough into a 3-inch circle and place 1 tablespoon meat mixture in the center of the circle. Lift up the edges of the circle and pinch 5 pleats up to create a pouch to encase the mixture. Pinch the top together. Repeat with the remaining slices of dough and filling. Make sure the dough is almost paper thin.

Heat a wok or nonstick skillet until very hot. Add 1 tablespoon vegetable oil, tilting the wok to coat the sides. If using a nonstick skillet, add 1/2 tablespoon vegetable oil. Place 12 dumplings in a single layer in the wok and fry 2 minutes, or until the bottoms are golden brown.

Add 1/2 cup water or broth. Cover and cook 6 to 7 minutes, or until the water is absorbed. Repeat with the remaining dumplings.

To make a dipping sauce, in a small bowl, mix the soy sauce with 1 teaspoon sesame oil. May add vinegar. Serve with the dumplings.

It all comes down to how they are cooked. While it is common to steam or pan-fry dumplings, cooks use both methods to make potstickers. The filled dumplings are pan-fried on one side and then steamed in broth or water. Properly made, the potstickers are crisp and browned on the bottom, sticking lightly to the pan, but easy to remove with a spatula.

The trick to making potstickers is not to overcook them, or they will live up to their name by sticking firmly to the pot! The right condiments can make potstickers taste even better. Here are several suggestions:

- Rice vinegar (red rice vinegar if possible)
- Soy sauce
- Shredded ginger

CIVIL WAR HARDTACK

Based on a Civil War Recipe:
Army Hardtack Recipe
Ingredients:
4 cups flour (preferably whole wheat)
4 teaspoons salt
Water (about 2 cups)
Optional and not in original recipe, ½ teaspoon soda
Pre-heat oven to 375° F
Makes about 10 pieces depending on how you size them.
Instructions
Mix the flour and salt together in a bowl. Add just enough water (less than two cups) so that the mixture will stick together, producing a dough that won't stick to hands or anything else.

<u>Mix the dough by hand.</u>

Roll the dough out, shaping it roughly into a rectangle. What I did was to roll it into a cookie sheet that had about a 1/2 in lip all the way round.

I cut the dough into rectangles and used a fork to punch holes in the tops. Like what you see with crackers.

Bake for 30 minutes. Turn each piece over and bake for another 30 minutes. The crackers should be slightly brown on both sides.

Dry in oven with the door open.

QUESO BLANCO CHEESE

<u>Ingredients:</u>

1 gallon whole milk

1/4 cup vinegar (I used apple cider vinegar-it doesn't matter if it has "mother" or not-any vinegar has the acid to work. Different types of vinegar may give slightly different flavors)

Yield: 1 1/2 -- 2 pounds

<u>Directions</u>

1. In a large pot, directly heat the milk to between 185 and 190 degrees F, stirring often to prevent scorching.

2. Slowly add the vinegar, a little at a time, until the curds separate from the whey. Usually 1/4 cup of vinegar will precipitate 1

gallon of milk. You may increase the temperature to 200 degrees F in order to use less vinegar and avoid an acidic or sour taste in your cheese. (Do not boil, as boiling will impart a "cooked" flavor.)

3. Ladle the curds into a colander lined with butter muslin. Tie the corners of the muslin into a knot and hang the bag to drain for several hours, or until the cheese has reached the desired consistency.

4. Remove the cheese from the muslin. Store in a covered bowl in the refrigerator for up to 2 weeks. Cheese does not melt, can be cut in cubes and added to stir fry or toasted. Can be used like Tofu. It also can be mashed and used in cottage Cheese Pie or Pudding recipes.

PLAIN ITALIAN SAUSAGE

15 pounds meat and suet
2 ounces salt (8 T)
1 cup smoked salt, plain salt works, lightly smoke finished sausages for smoke flavor
1 ounce ground black pepper (4 T)

1 ounce ground coriander (4 T)
¼ ounce mace (1T)
Mix with hands at least 15 minutes. A small amount of ice water may be added to make mixing easier. Pack into a pan and cool overnight. Grind through smaller plate of grinder once or twice. Stuff into casings. Boil in plain water until sausage floats, cool. Instead of stuffing, may use as bulk sausage.

How To Make Natural Glue Using Milk

Ingredients
1½ cups milk
3 tsp white vinegar
1 tbsp baking soda
Water by preference for thinning glue

Directions
1. Heat the milk in a pan until warm, then add vinegar.
2. Keep heating and stirring until the milk separates into curds and whey.
3. Strain the mixture, keeping the solid curds (save your whey for other uses!).
4. Collect the curds and put them back into the pan.
5. Add baking soda and enough water to get the consistency of your choosing and mix/stir thoroughly.

6. Heat the mixture until it starts bubbling a bit, then turn it off and let it cool.

7. Bottle in airtight container upon cooling enough and/or use it right away for gluing!

PLAYDOUGH (For the kids)

Mix 4 cups flour, 1 T. alum, ½ cup salt, set aside. Mix together, stirring constantly, 3 T. cooking oil, 2 cups boiling water, enough food color to make it look as dark as final color you want. Add to dry mix. Knead until smooth, Keep in well sealed container. Zip-close bags are fine. Does not need refrigerated.

POTATO DOUGHNUTS

Boil 3 large peeled potatoes, mash well and while still hot add 1 large T. butter and 2 cups sugar, beat well. Add 2 cups milk, 3 beaten eggs, 4 heaping t. baking powder, pinch of salt and 1 t. nutmeg, mix well, add enough flour to make soft dough. Start with 2 ½ cups flour. Dough should be soft but not sticky. Roll or pat out on floured board to ½ inch thick, cut with doughnut cutter or into bars. Carefully put into deep hot fat and turn at once. Cook until done, drain, roll in sugar or frost.

SODA CRACKERS (Saltines)

Mix 4 cups flour, ½ t. baking soda and 1 t. salt. Add 1 cup shortening or margarine. Add 3/4 cup sour milk, makes stiff dough. Knead thoroughly for 10 minutes. Roll out 1/4 inch or less, thick. Cut into squares, punch holes with fork, place on greased cookie sheet. Bake at 400 degrees until lightly browned. May sprinkle lightly with salt before baking, for saltines.

HONEY GRAHAM CRACKERS

<u>Mix together:</u>

¾ cup butter

½ cup honey

1 t. vanilla

Sift together and add to the above

<u>Ingredients:</u>

3 cups graham or whole wheat flour

½ cup wheat germ

½ t. baking powder
Cover and chill several hours or overnight.
Divide dough in half and place each half on a
small greased cookie sheet. Roll out dough
with a flour covered rolling pin until dough
covers each sheet in a thin layer, about ¼ to
1/8 inch thick. Try to be uniform for the
whole sheet and as even as possible on the
edges. Cut into squares and prick each square
at least 3 times with a fork. Bake at 325
degrees F. about 30 minutes. May add 1 t.
cinnamon to the dry ingredients before
combining with the rest or sprinkle on top
before baking.

Dutch Apple Dumplings

Recipe makes 4 dumplings.
1/2 c firmly packed dark brown sugar
3/4 c water
1 Tbsp butter, plus 4 more tsp
4 apples, peeled and cored
2 Tbsp raisins
4 tsp light brown sugar
cinnamon

your favorite pie dough, enough for a single crust pie

1. Preheat oven to 350 degrees. Make syrup: Place dark brown sugar, water and 1 tablespoon of butter in a small saucepan and bring to a boil. Reduce heat and simmer for a minute or two, to thicken up. Set aside.

2. Evenly divide raisins, light brown sugar and butter among the 4 apple core holes. Sprinkle all 4 apples with cinnamon.

3. Divide your chilled pie dough into 4 equal parts. Roll or hand flatten each into a "pancake" large enough to cover a whole apple. Place each apple in the center of its own round of dough. For each one, bring up the sides of the dough to cover and close in the apple. Place apples on a rimmed baking sheet, baste with syrup and bake for 20-25 minutes, basting 2-3 more times, until golden brown.

How To Clean Silver with Aluminum Foil

Clean all of your silver at once! Line your sink with aluminum foil, add 1/2 cup table salt, 1/2 cup baking soda, fill with hot water, then dump in all your silver! Let sit for about 30 min. The tarnish all transfers to the foil!

SWEETENED CONDENSED MILK

Combine 3/4 cup sugar, 1/3 cup evaporated milk and 2 T. margarine or butter in saucepan. Heat only until sugar is dissolved, stirring constantly. Use in any recipe calling for sweetened condensed milk.

EGGS

For anyone that may not know, the BEST way to make "hard-boiled" eggs is in the OVEN! Place the eggs in a muffin tray so they do not move around, turn the oven to 325 degrees, pop in for about 25-30 minutes and remove! Not only are they tastier, but they also are much easier to peel!
Bacon is easier to cook in the oven, also. Uniformly crispy without raw or overdone areas.

GRAFTING

You don't need grafting for apples, all you need is a fresh cutting and some rooting hormone. If you don't want to purchase rooting hormone, just grind up the bark from a handful of weeping willow branches and soak it in water for a few days. Make a fresh angled cut on your apple tree cutting and soak the cut end in the water overnight, then plant it in starter. Cut whatever leaves you have on the cutting in half and keep the plant misted and watered for a few weeks while it grows it's own roots.

Other books by Rosalyn Stowell

The Beginning
An Alaskan PAW Novel
Written by Mrs. Rosalyn E. Stowell

This is a stand alone Book 1 in a Trilogy. It is situated in Alaska and written by someone that actually lives in Alaska and knows the climate and differences.

226 pages
ISBN/EAN13:
0615752470 / 9780615752471   ISBN-13: 978-0615752471 (Custom Universal)
ISBN-10: 0615752470
BISAC: Fiction / Romance / Suspense

The Dark of Night
An Alaskan PAW Novel
Written by Mrs. Rosalyn E. Stowell

This is stand alone book 2 in a Trilogy.
218 pages
R. E.\Stowell
ISBN-13: 978-0615760780 (Custom Universal)
ISBN-10: 0615760783
BISAC: Fiction / Romance / Suspense

ALASKAN GOLD
Non Illegitimus Carborundum
An Alaskan Novel
Written By Rosalyn Stowell

A spur of the moment decision to check out her inheritance in person just might be the best thing to ever happen or maybe not. Why won't ex-fiancés stay ex'd and how do you tell Toads from the Prince's? An ex Fiance' that refuses to admit he is an ex, an Attorney that is not looking for long term, an Environmentalist looking to shut down mining and the boy next door. How to choose?. Set in Alaska, maybe 20 years ago or so, join Jo as she learns about living, mining and loving in the Bush, not always in that order.

My cookbook. Over 30 years in the making.

Don't
Use
A
Chainsaw
In The Kitchen!!

Cabin Etiquette or Harmony in the Bush

1. Always go outside to cut frozen meat, if you are using a chainsaw.
2. If you open it, close it.
3. If you break it, admit it.
4. If you can't fix it, find someone who can, or replace it.
5. If it wasn't given to you or you didn't buy or make it, it's not yours, leave it alone.
6. Always leave some firewood for the next person.
7. If you make a mess, clean it up.
8. If you're sorry, say so.
9. If you kill something, clean it.
10. Leave everything in better condition than you found it.
11. If you value it, take care of it.
12. If you turn it on, turn it off.
13. If you borrow it, return it.
14. If you move it, put it back.
15. If it belongs to someone else, get permission to use it.

Rosalyn Stowell

8.5" x 11" (21.59 x 27.94 cm)
Black & White on White paper
260 pages
R.E.Stowell
ISBN-13: 978-0615724324 (Custom Universal)
ISBN-10: 0615724329
BISAC: Cooking / Methods / Canning & Preserving
Over 400 recipes and assorted how-to
directions, on butchering, making sausage,
building a trappers cabin, tanning hides and
my autobiography at the back of the book.

About the writer:

I live 40 miles beyond phone or power lines. Over 50 miles beyond mail delivery. No TV, no radio, no door to door salesmen or politicians. Also no running water. It makes life simpler and a lot more fun. Of course, there is also no trash pickup or sidewalks. However, what there is, is a life full of interesting things to do and I have never been bored, ever.

I have lived in Alaska since 1969. I am a widow. I've operated heavy equipment, cooked, been a goldsmith, a taxidermist and a Registered Guide. I've built cabins and houses, waited tables, (very briefly, something to do with a pitcher of ice water and a customer) and peeled logs, painted pictures and worked as an artist's model to buy food and clothes for my children. I've even chauffeured for a while. I have held licenses as Boiler Operator, Taxidermist, Mill Operator, Registered Hunting Guide, Fishing Guide and for Mining. Life is interesting so be prepared for anything. You never know what is going to happen next.